THURSDAYS WITH MOSES

A Really Old Man, a Baby Boomer, and God's Great Lessons

Brad Densmore

Lamppost Library & Resource Center
Christ United Methodist Church
4488 Poplar Avenue
Memphis, Tennessee 38117

PROMISE PRESS
An Imprint of Barbour Publishing

© 2002 by Brad Densmore

The author is represented by BigScore Productions, Inc., 1986 Pickering Trail, Lancaster, PA 17601.

ISBN 1-58660-724-3

All rights reserved. No part of this publication may be reproduced or transmitted in any form or by any means without written permission of the publisher.

Published by Promise Press, an imprint of Barbour Publishing, Inc., P.O. Box 719, Uhrichsville, Ohio 44683, www.promisepress.com

ecpa Member of the
Evangelical Christian
Publishers Association

Printed in the United States of America.

5 4 3 2 1

chapter one

TEL AVIV

"THE KEY TO THE FUTURE OF EVERY LIVING PER-
SON IN ISRAEL'S RACE WAS BELIEVED TO EXIST IN
THESE TWO HEBREW ARTIFACTS."

Dr. Julius Goldberg, the curator, was addressing our tour group of twelve adults at the Eretz Israel Museum on Haim Levanon Street in Tel Aviv. "The Old Testament book of Exodus names them the Urim and the Thummim, and they were to be placed in the breastplate of Moses' brother Aaron, the priest, when he went before the Lord. The vestment was worn over Aaron's heart as he sat in judgment of Israel, possibly symbolic of God holding His people in His own heart.

"But there's more. Later, in the book of Numbers, Moses consulted God about the need for assistance with the obligations of leadership, and God instructed him to have Eleazar the priest install Joshua as a sort of vice president, if you will. Eleazar was to confer with God through the Urim. A holy response would be received, communicating God's decision.

"Finally, in the book of Deuteronomy, we find Moses

blessing the priestly line of Levi, saying that these oracles should remain with the high priest. The ancient Israelites believed these objects had extraordinary powers associated with God.

"Various archaeologists have searched for the Urim and Thummim over the last two hundred years, and some became skeptical that they ever existed. Of course, by now most of you are probably familiar with the story of the three children who just last summer were building a sand castle on the Mediterranean beach at Netanya, a short drive to our north. Digging deep for sand, they inadvertently uncovered the large clay pot holding what have now, at least unofficially, been determined to be the Urim and the Thummim. I submit, ladies and gentlemen, that you are within two meters of one of the most significant biblical discoveries of all time."

I was mesmerized. My own questions concerning the legendary powers proposed by Old Testament tradition had inspired me to research the topic for my master's thesis. Having received a small grant and my wife's reluctant permission, I was now face-to-face with two of the most fabled relics I'd hoped to study.

I admit I had doubts, and my left brain told me that a little skepticism was a healthy ally in proceeding with this kind of investigation. Yet these small somethings seemed to stare at me like a rankled John Wayne: "Don't look now, pilgrim, but there might be an ambush up at the pass." I shut down the thought and began scratching notes on my yellow legal pad, reminding myself that my paper would never get finished if I allowed my imagination to fire up.

Jockeying to get nearer to the protective glass enclosure, I nudged a pretty young lady with black flowing hair and almond-shaped eyes, who responded to my "Sorry" with a wince. *It's a small price to pay for getting within an arm's length of the prize,* I told myself.

The Urim and Thummim looked like oversized hatpins, no more than five inches long but amazingly ornate. The first—a slight majority of experts claim it was the Urim—was made of copper, about the diameter of a pencil, crowned with the head of a winsome, Helen-of-Troy-looking woman. The metal stem had reverted to verdigris. There was debate about restoring it, but for now it would remain as it was discovered.

The other was brass, and its adorning feature was the head of a bull. I deemed the artisan meticulous, brilliant even, as I read an expression of authority on the animal's diminutive face. Magic powers or not, seeing these pieces was worth the price of my plane ticket to Israel.

"May we take pictures?" I asked our host.

"Be our guest," he answered.

My eyes still glued to these engaging historical treasures, I reached down to unzip my camera case and extricate my Nikon. But something wasn't right. My legs began to wobble, and a dull rumble sounded, mimicking the approach of a fast-moving Amtrak train; yet I hadn't remembered seeing any railroad tracks nearby.

The rumble quickly swelled to a strong vibration, then a shaking, and the accompanying roar created an ominous cacophony.

"Earthquake!" someone shouted. Pandemonium! The structure began thrashing like a mosh pit at a Nine Inch

Nails concert. I didn't think I could run. Debris started falling, and the others were scattering frantically toward the exits. I watched helplessly as the woman I had bumped earlier stumbled. In the eternity of the next split second, I thought of my wife and family and decided I had to survive.

Rrrrrrrrrrr. The museum's alarm began to mourn the tectonic attack as I fell to my knees, unable to ride the concrete waves any longer. I turned to my left just in time to see the entire exhibit falling toward me.

The artifacts! With a horrific crash, the impeccably crafted cabinet dove to a violent death, sprinkling its glass and disgorging its priceless treasure not two feet from where I was huddled. Without thought, I managed to reach out and scoop up the Urim and Thummim, one in each hand. But as I transferred the greenish object to my right hand, the two collided, igniting a shower of sparks like a welding rod jabbing its metallic prey. My fingers felt as if I'd grabbed a handful of the sun, and I was choking in smoke. My consciousness took a sabbatical.

chapter two

AMMON

"LIFE MOVES AT A MUCH SLOWER PACE HERE IN 1398 B.C. AMMON, BUT THAT'S NOT TO SAY NOTHING IS HAPPENING. THE ISRAELITES, AFTER MEANDERING AROUND IN THE SINAI PENINSULA FOR THE LAST FORTY YEARS, GIVE OR TAKE A WEEK, ARE PREPARING TO BATTLE FOR THE MILK AND HONEY OF CANAAN, THE PROMISED LAND. MOST OF THE ORIGINAL PARTY WHO LEFT EGYPT UNDER THE DESPOTIC AND VENGEFUL EYE OF THE EGYPTIAN PHARAOH HAVE DIED. THEIR CHILDREN AND GRANDCHILDREN ARE NOW POISED TO CLAIM THE HOMELAND THEIR FATHERS WILL NEVER SEE."

The narrator's voice sounded familiar, yet strange. "Dr. Goldberg? Dr. Goldberg?" I called out. No reply. *What did he say? Ammon…1398 B.C.? What's going on? What in heaven's name is going on?* I sat up and looked around, scanning the landscape for anything familiar. No museum. No Tel Aviv. Only vast expanses of nothing.

Flattening my palms to the ground to raise myself, a miniature lightning bolt shot through my right hand. I immediately dropped back down, raising my hand and turning it to my face for inspection. A burned ridge running tangent to my lifeline was enough to startle the facts back to my clearing mind. The Urim and Thummim were no longer in my possession, but as I turned, something yellow came into view on the ground behind me—my legal pad. The pen was sleeping quietly beneath it.

An uncanny sense of where I was and what was taking place now pervaded my brain, and it struck me that I was a spectator, a foreign correspondent of sorts, with my life and spirit still rooted firmly in twenty-first-century America. There, the biggest news was terrorism and Wall Street, with the new perpetrators of evil bearing names like Enron and WorldCom.

In the aftermath of the globe-wrenching technology stock meltdown, New York City and Washington, D.C. had suffered ineffable blows at the hands of madmen. Yet the fundamental greed of a handful of the far-too-rich remained unaltered, and good people were paying a price. Now these events existed only in my mind. America would not be thought of for another three thousand years; even the creative book cooking of Arthur Andersen's finest could not change that.

I'd barely gotten to my feet and walked a dozen yards when I spotted a Zacchaeus-sized man. (I was wearing sunglasses, a T-shirt, and Levis. It occurred to me that someone might spot the label and take me for a priest, but no such luck.) With a voice like Tattoo, he began shouting, "Alien! Alien! Stone him!"

"Wait!" I countered instinctively, as the vertically challenged Hebrew approached with three of his lackeys. True to form, I followed with the first ridiculous cliché that popped into my head: "I'm here to see your leader. I've been sent by God." Although I didn't say it with the conviction of Dan Aykroyd in *The Blues Brothers,* it sufficed. They would take me to their leader—and their leader was Moses.

My mind now fell victim to a *coup d'état* of childhood Sunday school flashbacks. As a kid, my imagination could quickly fill in all the gaps (a task not as easily completed at age forty-five): Moses, standing at the edge of the Red Sea, arms in a Zeus-like stretch, separating the waves like giant, greenish gray theater curtains; and legions of Israelites following in disbelief, traipsing across benign puddles where millions of gallons of ominous seawater had tossed just moments before.

And of course, there was Charlton Heston. As if by godly edict, Mr. DeMille etched his own version of Moses into our Western minds with the same "Finger of Jehovah" that inscribed the Ten Commandments in stone. Hollywood has a penchant for choosing entertainment over truth; yet its depictions of these people and events are not easily erased from our memories.

Ammon is a hilly region. The peaks don't challenge the fourteen-thousand-plus summits of the Rockies by any means, but Mount Nebo tops out around twenty-seven hundred feet, so it's not like a hike around my home in southern Michigan.

I was now perspiring heavily as we climbed an obstinate hill, my Reeboks attempting to shape themselves to the uneven rocks beneath. The fiery afternoon sun reminded me of Aruba, but there was a noticeable difference: no water. I was wishing I'd worn a hat. *Maybe something like my Air Jordan baseball cap,* I thought to myself.

The physical challenge had probably been good for me, and as we approached the peak, I was occupied with keeping my balance as well as staying mentally focused. I had said nothing further to my traveling companions since beginning this jaunt, knowing they were holding far more cards than I. Someone once said it's better to remain quiet and be thought a fool, than to open your mouth and remove all doubt. (It seemed like good advice, and the thought occurred to me that if I brought this up to Moses, it might be left for Solomon to ponder in another four centuries or so!) Besides, for the moment I had these men convinced that I was an angel, and I reveled at being in the company of Michael Landon, John Travolta, and Roma Downey. I wondered if I might end up in the Bible after all. Attempting to amuse myself with all this, we reached the summit.

I could not have prepared myself psychologically for what now filled my gaze: a sea, but not the Red Sea. This was a sea of tents, people, livestock, more tents, more people, more animals—the Hebrew version of urban sprawl, magnified exponentially.

Before I knew it, we were running the gauntlet, my escorts carelessly pushing aside children, goats, and anything that obstructed our trail to the tent of their legendary helmsman.

Every face I encountered stared back at me like I was the Elephant Man, and I suddenly felt a baseball in the pit of my stomach. We passed bearded old men, arguing children, wagons with crocks stacked above and people sleeping beneath. We stopped suddenly.

The tent was crude but generous. It appeared to have been made from the stretched hides of various animals, and the shades of browns and grays reflected the landscape that was a backdrop to the camp. My captors talked with a youthful-appearing man (whom I presumed to be a bodyguard), whose piercing dark eyes seemed to penetrate my soul. I attempted a smile but failed. My legs were now rubbery, and I doubt that I could have spoken if I'd wanted to.

Thwap! The door flaps of the primitive domicile curled out briskly. Two large, serious-looking, robe-clad men quickly positioned themselves on either side of me, grasped my arms just above the elbows, and led me forward. My Reeboks seemed to barely scrape the dirt. Pushing aside the crude curtains, we ducked into the tent of Moses.

The accommodations were spartan: a small array of crocks of various shapes and sizes scattered here and there, two small wooden barrels, and a rack with some garments hung over it. There were some cooking utensils and four piles of hides, apparently used for sparing the posteriors of the occupants from the hard desert ground.

I studied the items carefully, wanting desperately to remember every detail, yet fully cognizant of my potentially precarious situation. My fate now rested entirely on the response of the Old Testament's most celebrated hero.

When I was a very young boy, I believed in Santa Claus

SALES DRAFT

SUPERCUTS
6045 STAGE RD STE 60
BARTLETT, TN 38134
TERMINAL 1545021

0866000A
01/23/2009 11:09:31

EDS
XXXXXXXXXXXX9133
INVOICE 9600A DP2
AUTH. CODE 531266

SALE TOTAL $15.00

CUSTOMER COPY

```
            SALES DRAFT

               SUPERCUTS
          6045 STAGE RD STE 60
           BARTLETT, TN 38134
            TERMINAL 1545021

06660004
01/23/2009    11:09:31

EDS
    XXXXXXXXXXXX9133
INVOICE      96004 DP2
AUTH. CODE   531266

SALE TOTAL              $15.00

          CUSTOMER COPY
```

with every ounce of my being. I remember watching out the window of my upstairs bedroom, hoping beyond hope for a glimpse of that rutilant nose of the lead reindeer, the apple red sleigh, and the mystical-but-jovial man who epitomized happiness, generosity, impartiality, and, of course, magic. The only thing that stood between a sighting and me was my child-weariness. I never saw the *real* Santa Claus. Almost as important to my childish mind was Moses—and here, decades later, was the chance to validate a part of child-hood that I feared might be forever gone.

"Stand up. Who are you?" The command startled me since I didn't remember dropping to my knees. Focusing as I rose, I realized I was looking into the face of Moses.

He was old. I recalled the biblical account attributing him 120 years, and a stooped posture sentineled by a ruggedly wrinkled face suggested he might be close to that. Had he been able to stand straight, he would have approached six feet, but now my own five-foot seven-inch frame was sufficient for a level look into his storied eyes. I had arrived for the final chapter of his life, and with this realization, a melancholy spirit prodded me.

"Who are you?" he repeated, as I once again felt powerful hands gripping my biceps.

"My name is…Br…Brad," I responded, collecting myself.

"You have light-colored skin. Where are you from?"

"Well, it's, uh, a little bit complicated." I hesitated. "It may be difficult for you to believe."

"Listen, young man," he retorted, "I've seen rods turned into serpents, rivers changed to blood, and attacks by locusts and flies. I watched the Red Sea part, and I brought the Ten Commandments down from the holy mountain after witnessing God etch them in stone. Now do you really think I'll have a problem believing where you're from, or do I need to continue?"

"No, sir. I understand," I responded, fighting to restrain a reflexive smile that attempted to sneak across my face.

Did he know that I already knew about those events? There was certainly a tone of astuteness in his voice, like a general who had experienced the horrors of war and would not be fooled. His deep brown eyes, garnished with brows of dark gray and silver-white, reflected wisdom commensurate with his many years.

"Do you?" The old commander demanded his due.

"Yes," I said, acquiescing. With that, Moses nodded at the two men who constrained me, and they released their potent grip on my arms, turned, and exited the tent.

"Come and sit down," he ordered. I felt twenty pounds lighter as I traced the old sage's short steps to the rear of the tent. Motioning toward a large, rust-orange clay crock, he continued, "There's the wine, and the cups are in that barrel. I'm certain you're thirsty."

"Thank you. I am." Reaching down into the barrel, I retrieved two drinking vessels, which appeared to be made of glass, the hazy greenish color that shows up in the western sky just before the awful, late spring storm that wipes out the trailer park. The wine jug appeared too full and heavy to lift and pour safely, and I was unsure of ancient Hebrew etiquette. Moses now had his back to me, so I quickly dipped the cups into the crock, filling them both about three-quarters full, then wiping the residue on my shirt.

Moses positioned himself on what looked like a heap of faded curtains, contorted into a ball the size of a small ottoman, a primordial overstuffed chair. He meticulously adjusted the mature cloth, then sighed like a tired farmer who had just spent fourteen hours baling hay on a hot day. I held out one of the cups. A withering hand clasped it and drew it to his lips.

I sat not three feet away on a braided rug, badly worn and faded but offering hints that it may have been a spectacular garnishment in its day. I tasted the wine. My mouth was parched from my journey, and I found no Pepsi machines on the way. Neither did my captors show any interest in my personal comfort. This grape juice was warm, but sweet and welcome—and it was courtesy of Moses. I knew what was coming.

"Son," he began, "tell me your story."

"Well, Moses...may I call you Moses?" I queried, unsure of my place.

"That's what people have been calling me ever since Pharaoh's daughter found my crib-ark floating in the Nile. Actually, the Hebrew name is *Mosheh,* but for English, *Moses* is fine."

"That's something that's been bothering me," I blurted.

"What's that?"

"Everyone here is speaking English!"

"Do you speak any Hebrew?" Moses asked.

"Not a word."

"Then I'd say you got lucky, didn't you?"

When I had first tasted the wine, I was reasonably certain it hadn't fermented. Now I wasn't quite sure.

"I guess so," I mumbled, then stated straightforwardly, "I'm from the future." I was resigned to the fact that I could not lie my way out of the situation. Besides, if this man of such monumental historical and religious significance was going to trust me, the least I could do was be honest. Moses, regardless of his advanced years, was still the law of this land. Whatever was going to happen to me would be at his pleasure.

He seemed to stare through me for several minutes before finally breaking the deafening silence. "The future? When and where in the future?" His apparent acceptance startled me.

"About three thousand years, in a country called the United States of America. It's about 7,000 miles west of here or 18,000 miles east. It just depends which way you go around."

"Around?"

Now I was in trouble. It dawned on me that as recently as the seventeenth century Galileo had been threatened with death for postulating that the earth rotated around the sun. I was now in a civilization two-plus millennia prior, and a round earth was not kosher here. I quickly settled on a gambit.

"Sorry. Where I come from, we say *get around* meaning *to go from place to place.*" I answered convincingly enough to fool even a polygraph machine. Another silence followed.

"Do you know, then, what will be the future of my race, the outcome of our battle for Canaan?"

"We have accounts. We have a collection of writings re-ferred to as the Old Testament and archeological objects."

"And...?" Moses paused, then turned slowly away from me. Turning back, he mouthed the word *no,* and began shaking his ahead slowly. "It is in the hands of God. We've come too far; this is another test of my faith." I smiled at Moses and nodded. This was no fool.

"So, Brad, do you know why you are here?"

"I can't say for certain."

"But you have an idea."

"Only a hunch, Moses. I'd like to spend time with you, learn from you. I'd like to somehow get your wisdom back to the world of my time. It's the only possible reason I can think of for my ending up here."

Moses smiled a broad, satisfied smile, like a geriatric actor who'd just won a lifetime-achievement award at the Oscars. A part of me wanted to stay there, in that time, in that tent, in that moment.

"And that yellow papyrus—is that for writing?" he questioned, referring to my legal pad.

"It is. And there's enough paper here to accommodate many of your thoughts, Moses, if you agree," I assured.

"Well then, my futuristic friend, so shall it be," he announced with regal certainty. "But I have much to attend to before I go to my final rest. You may stay in a tent nearby and help tend the herds and flocks while you sojourn with us. Come and see me every Thursday, and we'll spend time talking."

"Thursday? Is there significance to that?" I asked.

"It's the day after hump day," he declared matter-of-factly.

"Hump day...as in over the hump of the workweek?" I queried.

"No. Hump day as in the day we water the camels."

chapter three

THE FIRST THURSDAY:

WE TALK ABOUT WANDERING

MY FIRST DAYS TENDING THE FLOCKS IN THE MID-
SPRING HEAT OF AMMON GAVE ME A NEW APPRE-
CIATION FOR THE TRADE, AND WHEN I JUXTAPOSED
THE LIVES OF THESE PEOPLE WITH THE LIVES OF
MY TWENTY-FIRST-CENTURY COUNTERPARTS IN
AMERICA, I HAD TO OPT FOR THE CUSHINESS OF
POSTMODERN CIVILIZATION.

The few Israelites I spoke with looked upon me
strangely, to be sure, but my ordination as a friend of Moses
elevated me to a position of respect. I was given the custo-
mary wardrobe, and while this was a major step in assimi-
lating, I was thankful that cameras didn't exist; I looked like
a Deuteronomic dork. At least my sunglasses were a trendy
accent.

I approached Moses' tent at midmorning. I had arrived on
a Sunday—not to be confused with the Hebrew Sabbath,
which is Saturday. I was therefore definitely grateful to only
have endured three days of my new antiquated lifestyle prior
to our first official meeting. The highlights of those days

included prolonged stares from my new hosts, removing the doo-doo of various animals from my sandals, and getting used to life without running water and watching *The West Wing* and the eleven o'clock news before going to bed.

My presence was immediately announced, and Moses called for me to enter. Despite the loss of modern comforts, I felt incredibly special. He seemed anxious to begin, and I quickly found my nest.

"Brad," he chimed, with the vitality of a much younger man, "I'd like to talk about wandering. Do you know how long it's taken us to get here since we left Egypt?"

I interpreted the question as rhetorical and remained silent.

"Over forty years. And we've lost tens of thousands of people. It all seems so unnecessary, and I have to believe it could have been avoided."

"You were at the border of Canaan just a few weeks after you left Mount Sinai, weren't you?" I inquired, trying to recall the story from the book of Numbers.

"You know about that?" Moses countered, apparently surprised.

"Remember? I mentioned we have accounts," I followed, with as much diplomacy as I could muster. "Moses, you're going to be written about; you must know that."

"I have some men writing things now," he admitted. "They seem good for little else: wouldn't last ten minutes in battle and are generally too lazy to help with the live-stock. They mainly bother the women at night and then sleep till the sun is high in the sky. We have several ways to punish those who don't carry their weight here—I guess

I've been pretty lenient so far."

"Canaan, Moses. You were at the border of Canaan."

"Right. I sent out twelve spies to investigate the land, one man from each tribe. I always figured that representation was important, and these people were always looking for something to complain about as it was. Anyway, two of the men, Joshua and Caleb, came back with fresh fruit—you know, grapes, figs, pomegranates—and I thought, *This is it!*

"They also said that the cities were fortified so we would encounter resistance, but they seemed convinced it was within our grasp. The other ten men returned, saying the land was inhabited by giants, that we looked like grasshoppers in comparison, and that Lot's wife would come back to life before we would take Canaan."

I bowed my head, planted my nose in the palm of my left hand, and spread my fingers across my face.

"So we retreated. And now, here we are again, after forty years. Forty years! The point is, there is no opportunity that doesn't involve risk, and sacrifice is always part of the package. We surely might have lost many men, but we lost them anyway, dying of old age and disease in the desert. I can't see that there's anything nobler about that. Can you?"

"But don't you have to give credence to the ten spies versus two?" I interjected as he paused.

"Ox-puckey!" he crackled. "The majority is usually wrong. The majority is made up of cowards. It's typically the odd man out who bears listening to."

I thought about life at home, the people I knew. Many were once close to their own promised land of sorts: a dream, a plan. But they listened to the majority who told them it wouldn't work, that their scheme would devour them. So they wander, never quite getting where they want to go.

Moses read my mind. "Too many men are wanderers, Brad. For most of them, it's easier to meander through a desert, complaining, always blaming God or someone else. All because they didn't have the courage or good sense to ignore the naysayers and seize the moment when it was staring them in the face."

Lamppost Library & Resource Center
Christ United Methodist Church
4488 Poplar Avenue
Memphis, Tennessee 38117

chapter four

THE SECOND THURSDAY:

WE TALK ABOUT THE LAW

I WAS BEGINNING TO MAKE FRIENDS WITH A COUPLE OF MY FELLOW HERDSMEN. I HAD VOWED TO MOSES NOT TO REVEAL MY SECRET OR OUR PROJECT, SO ALL THAT CONVERSATION WAS OFF-LIMITS. BUT I DISCOVERED THAT EBADIAH AND IDBASH HAD A GENUINE DESIRE TO SHARE THEIR OPINIONS WITH ME, AND IT PROBABLY DIDN'T HURT THAT I TREATED THEM AS IF THEY WERE GENIUSES. THEY WERE YOUNG MEN, PROBABLY IN THEIR MIDTWENTIES, WHO DID HAVE SOMETHING TO OFFER. AS I LISTENED TO THEIR STORIES AND DREAMS OF THE COMING CONQUEST, I FOUND MYSELF APPRECIATING THEM MORE AND MORE. THE DAYS PASSED RATHER QUICKLY. THURSDAY ARRIVED, AND IT WAS TIME TO MEET WITH MOSES ONCE AGAIN.

"What's the most important consideration for your race now?" I asked, after Moses' perfunctory greetings.

"That's an easy one!" he responded without pausing.
"The Law. Without respect for these ideas, we're doomed.
I've been observing human beings for over a hundred
years, and I firmly believe the masses must respect fundamental rules, or civilization will fall apart. What about in
your time? Does the world have laws three thousand years
from now?"

"Definitely," I answered. "Our country has a constitution
and thousands of laws."

"How is it working?"

"We're still killing each other, but, generally speaking, it
works reasonably well."

Moses looked hard at me. "I'm saddened," he said with a
resigned passion, "but I'm not surprised. Killing comes from
the part of a man that he is at once most proud of and most
ashamed of. Our sixth commandment says, 'Don't kill'; yet
when we go into Canaan, we know that we will kill and be
killed. But we believe God has sent us to claim the land,
and we really have few options."

"And what about murder among your own people?"

"It happens. Squabbles over property, livestock, wives, you
name it. We've tried to address all of this as best we can, but
we just end up chiseling more laws into stone. We already
have three carts full of legal tablets. Frankly, I'm tired of laws.
If people would just use a little decency and common sense,
we could make those oxen a lot happier.

"But..." he began with renewal, as if realizing he was soft-
ening, "until I see some evidence of that, I'll continue to
emphasize where we've come from, what we've survived, and
the value of the Law in seeing us through."

"My herdsmen friends have been telling me you also have lots of laws about what people are allowed to eat," I said. "I can't help but be curious about that."

"God told Aaron and me that He wanted us Hebrews to be unique among nations and that one way to accomplish this was to acknowledge some distinction of diet. One animal we don't eat is swine, mainly because pigs have been used in pagan rituals for a long time, and we're not to be associated with that sort of thing. We're forbidden from eating camels as well, and although this is just my theory, I have a feeling that God wants to make sure we preserve our transportation."

"Don't eat your ride," I couldn't resist quipping.

Moses looked at me somewhat quizzically, nodded, and continued, "Some of the other things, I believe, have caused sickness and disease, like moles and lizards; it just doesn't make sense to take the risk. But bear in mind, we have a cleansing process for those who violate these rules. It's not severe, but we do need to maintain who we are."

There was still something bothering me. "Moses," I posed sincerely, "when your people realize their dream, their mission, and inhabit the Promised Land, will there be less need for laws?"

"No, there will be *more* need," Moses responded philosophically. "Think about it. You've just told me you have thousands of laws in the future. Why is that? I'm guessing it's because you have much more to protect. If a man has little to lose, that man is generally unconcerned with laws. It is only when he believes he has something significant, something of great value, that he becomes persuaded of the importance of preserving and enjoying it.

"When we left Egypt, we had no home, but we were still a nation. We had family, livestock, and some chattel we carried out with us. As soon as we reached Mount Sinai, God gave us the Law. Why? I think to establish that what we currently possessed at that time had value. Our blessings from God, our newfound freedom, the people of our tribe, the hope for a new homeland, the animals and goods we still had—these had worth. So God gave us laws to say, 'Look, I understand how humans think, and they think valuable things need protection, so here it is. Now behave yourselves, and let's move ahead.' "

"Yet you still think there's a better way," I suggested.

"You know it, I know it, and don't think for a minute that God doesn't know it. But the three of us are also tuned in to human nature. I have a feeling in these old bones that if you traveled three thousand years ahead of your time, you could still talk with people about laws."

Back in my tent that evening, I pondered Moses' words. The essence of the book of Deuteronomy, I recalled, was a recounting and expanding of the original Law. If Moses hadn't made the speeches recorded in that book, he would soon. Yet all that was needed to replace three oxcarts full of inscribed stone tablets was "a little decency and common sense." I couldn't help but ruminate about the world I came from and the indescribably horrific events in New York City and Washington, D. C., now overshadowing the tragedies of Oklahoma City, Columbine, and Waco. Decency and common sense floundered in my mind like a helpless fish washed up on an empty beach. Finally, I succumbed to a restless sleep.

31

THURSDAYS WITH MOSES

chapter five

THE THIRD
THURSDAY:

WE TALK ABOUT SLAVERY

My life as a historically challenged expatriate grew more intriguing as the days passed. I managed to bump into Joshua after less than a month in Ammon though I was leading a fairly sequestered life. He looked to be sixty-something, but with the physique of an ageless Greek god. Having been born into bondage in Egypt and serving as one of the original twelve spies who scouted Canaan forty years earlier, he was no stranger to peril or adversity. He possessed a charisma that seemed to surpass even that of Moses.

Joshua had apparently been given a few details regarding my mission, but he seemed genuinely interested in me aside from all that. He was on his way to see Moses when our paths crossed, so we walked the camp's dusty trail together for about a quarter of a mile. Arriving at the primitive shelter, Joshua asked me to remain outside while he went to see his revered teacher. I waited in the late spring heat for much longer than I had hoped. Finally, he exited the tent, assured me that we would talk again, and disappeared into the canvas community.

"Are you waiting patiently?" Moses called out in an almost singsong voice.

"You need a waiting room with some six-month-old copies of *USA Today,*" I joked.

"Whatever a 'waiting room' is," Moses countered. "Right now, we've got plenty of waiting going on. And I have no idea what *USA Today* is all about."

"You have plenty of company," I said. "It might be best to leave it at that."

The smell of Moses' accommodations was becoming familiar: the sweet violet fragrance of wine, the twice-stale odor of cloth garments that needed laundering, and the vernal, dusty, ubiquitous desert scent of this land that seemed doubly present here.

"What's on your mind today, Moses?" I asked respectfully.

"I've been thinking about slavery," he stated matter-of-factly. "Do you know about Pharaoh?"

"He had a reputation."

"He was an evil, contemptuous, and cruel man," Moses confirmed. "Many of my people died under the whips of his taskmasters. They were forced to build his storage cities from the ground up. They made the bricks, transported them, and constructed the buildings. In return, they were abused horribly. It's unthinkable to me that some of our people actually wanted to return to Egypt at the first sign of trouble."

"Fear of the unknown?" I inquired.

"Probably," he answered. "But Joshua and many of the others will tell you that bondage is much more than physical indignity. There's a spiritual imprisonment that's difficult to describe. Some have said there were times when they wondered if they were human, alive, *real.*"

"I can't imagine," I responded.

"Nor can I," Moses continued. "I was never actually enslaved. But I saw the devastation and havoc it wreaked upon my people. Even though I didn't feel qualified to be their leader, I realized something had to be done, and God forced my hand. This idea of one man owning another, denying him his own will and a chance to make a life for himself as he can—there's something wrong about that. It goes against nature."

"Nature?" I echoed. "But isn't nature itself cruel?"

"Absolutely," Moses agreed. "Surely you've observed that living things fall prey to other living things. Animals kill other animals for food, for survival. Sometimes, such as in war, men become victims of other men. But in those cases, death is immediate, even *liberating*. With slavery, you hold others against their will, slowly draining their life, their dreams, their desire to exist." He paused contemplatively.

"There's more, isn't there?" I asked, sensing something further.

"There are many kinds of slavery," he started again. "Human beings have often chosen bondage. In our history, we have the story of Adam and Eve, the first man and woman whom God created. They elected slavery through disobedience. I would hazard that most of us have managed to enslave ourselves in one way or another because of bad decisions. In a real sense, we've been slaves of the desert these last forty years because of our lack of faith in God and in ourselves."

"So why do you think God just doesn't step in and say, 'Here, everyone, here is your freedom. I'm giving it to you'?"

"I imagine He's hoping that eventually we'll get smart enough to figure it out for ourselves," he rejoined.

"Will God live that long?" I asked, smiling. Moses broke into a hearty, infectious laugh, and I followed. When the laughter subsided, the day's lesson was over.

I slept much better that night.

THURSDAYS WITH MOSES

chapter six

THE FOURTH THURSDAY:

WE TALK ABOUT SACRIFICES

I CONTINUED TO ASK QUESTIONS AND LEARN FROM MY HERDSMEN FRIENDS. EBADIAH INFORMED ME THAT WE WERE IN THE MONTH OF ABIB, AND WHILE I WAS AWARE IT WAS EARLY SPRINGTIME, I UNDERESTIMATED THE IMPORTANCE OF KNOWING THE MONTH. (LATER IN HISTORY, THE ISRAELITES WOULD DRAW UPON THE BABYLONIAN CALENDAR AND INSTITUTE THE NAME NISAN.) ABIB WAS THE MONTH WHEN PASSOVER WOULD BE COMMEMORATED, AND THE TIME WAS NEARLY UPON US.

"Come and be our guest for the celebration of our deliverance," Ebadiah requested with an uncommon grace.

"But I'm not from your nation," I answered. "Are you sure it would be all right?"

"You're circumcised, aren't you?" he asked, with no

40

hint of inappropriateness.

"I'd be happy to be your guest," I said, realizing I was more Hebrew than I thought.

Soon people began coming to our fields to select young sheep and goats, and our orders were simply to ask them how many would be sharing the meat. As long as their request seemed reasonable, we complied by providing perfect specimens. The families were to keep the animals alive for four days prior to the Passover feast, which was on the fourteenth day of Abib. A holy day and seven days of eating unleavened bread would follow this, I was told. My memory being a bit fuzzy on all the biblical details, I was being extremely careful about what I said; this was serious business here.

I also realized that I would be meeting again with Moses prior to the event. There was little doubt as to what our subject matter would be.

"I've been invited by one of my fellow herdsmen to share in the Passover feast," I told Moses, with a hint of reservation. "May I participate?"

"You're circumcised, aren't you?"

"If I didn't know better, I'd say there was a conspiracy."

"Your friend already confirmed it?" Moses almost smiled.

"He took my *word* for it," I clarified. "Moses, I know you've decided it's best not to ask me about the future, but I think you'll be pleased to know this little surgical procedure is still quite popular in my time. Do you find that surprising?"

"Not really. We do it to identify ourselves with God. Some things never lose their appeal." He did seem pleased.

"Tell me about Passover, Moses," I asked, hearing myself

sound like a seven-year-old Opie seeking eternal truth from the sheriff of Mayberry.

"The last plague that God brought upon Egypt before our deliverance from Pharaoh was the death of the firstborn. God told us that if we killed a young lamb or goat and put some of its blood above our doorways, our households would be spared from the angel of death. We did this and suffered no casualties.

"God thought it would be a good thing if we commemorated the event every year at this time so no one would forget—and the children would grow up knowing how He had protected us. Of course, there is a deeper significance as well to those who've come to understand it." Moses paused before continuing. "It's about sacrifice."

"Sacrifice of the animals?" I inquired.

"That's only symbolic," he countered. "Everything costs something. On the surface, the animals we eat at Passover lose their lives so we can be fed. But the blood we dab above our doorways signifies a substitution of animal blood for human blood. A lamb died, but our children's lives were spared. That's part of the greater lesson."

"I'm still a bit confused," I said.

"You'll understand in time," Moses assured me. "Just know that God sacrifices for His creation, and everyone who is like God must be unselfish in the same way. Good parents often deny themselves certain comforts to help their children. Genuine leaders may deprive themselves of personal success to allow their followers to become heroes. A teacher may appear ignorant while permitting his students to become wise. Nothing worthwhile is ever gained without exchange, without trading something of importance."

"I'll ponder this during Passover," I said.

Moses looked at me with an aging father's eyes. "So will I," he admitted.

Passover seemed to have a renewing and invigorating effect on this homeless nation camped east of the Jordan River. I was beginning to understand why. When my host shared the story of Pharaoh's relentless domination of the Hebrews and God's deliverance through plagues and miracles, Ebadiah's young son listened wide-eyed.

Reuben was six years old, olive-skinned and handsome, sporting thick, shiny-as-patent-leather hair. He was also proof that attention deficit disorder existed prior to the twenty-first century. Yet when the legendary tales began, he was entranced and sat perfectly still—seemingly his own antithesis—until Ebadiah finished the part about the Red Sea crossing and took a breath.

I was enchanted also. If this was going on throughout the community, and I had reason to believe it was, what a metamorphosis must be occurring. And although my narrator was a second-generation Hebrew born several years after the exodus, many around us were hearing accounts from those who had actually lived through these events.

The common thread was Moses: Moses the reluctant leader, Moses the persistent thorn in Pharaoh's flesh, Moses the obstinate lawgiver, and now Moses the aging philosopher. I ruminated on his words: *sacrifice, bondage, law, wandering. Never something for nothing, but always something for something.* Tonight it was blood for blood. I sat beside

Ebadiah's quiet-but-mindful, subservient wife and watched while father and son dipped their contrived sponge-on-a-stick into the lamb's blood and went outside the tent to mark their door. Now we were all safe.

chapter seven

THE FIFTH THURSDAY:

WE TALK ABOUT LEADERSHIP

THURSDAY ARRIVED QUICKLY—IN A DEAD HEAT WITH MY DESIRE TO MEET WITH MY AGING MENTOR. AS I APPROACHED THE TENT, I RECOGNIZED A FAMILIAR FORM: JOSHUA. THE LATE MORNING SUN CORUSCATED ACROSS HIS RUGGED FRAME, FREEZING AN IMAGE IN MY MIND THAT I COULD NOT HAVE CONJURED BY ANY POSSIBLE CEREBRAL MEANS. I'D NO SOONER COUNTED MYSELF INEFFABLY FORTUNATE THAN MOSES EXITED THE TENT, PUT HIS ARMS ON JOSHUA'S SHOULDERS, AND EMBRACED HIM. I WAITED, WATCHING FROM A DISTANCE. SOME MOMENTS IN TIME ARE NOT TO BE INTERRUPTED.

Their conversation was brief, and as soon as I saw Joshua begin to step back, I advanced toward them, hoping that I could obtain some hint as to the reason for his visit. Seeing me, Joshua called out.

"Greetings, friend." *Friend*. The word rang in my ears like an ethereal wind chime.

"Good morning, Joshua!" I exclaimed, sounding like a ten-year-old Chicago kid who'd just bumped into Michael Jordan. "It's great to see you."

"I have to leave now," he said apologetically, "but I'm coming to visit you soon. Where are you tending?"

"By the east ridge," I answered, "with Ebadiah and Idbash."

"I'll find you," he assured me, "in a few days."

"I'll look forward to it," I said, still somewhat in amazement. I stood beside Moses as we watched Joshua disappear into the morning's commotion.

"You're proud of him, aren't you?" I stated respectfully.

"Beyond words," Moses replied with all the pride of a father whose son had just graduated from West Point. "You know, I feel good about leaving him in charge of these people when I'm gone. He's proven over and over that he loves them. He cares about their future, and he has the courage to do what he knows is right."

"You can't ask more from a leader," I offered.

"Come inside," he ordered. "There's much more to say."

I pulled back the faded, brown fabric that covered the opening and held it for my Old Testament mentor. I followed into his tent.

"Leaders are often lonely people," Moses shared as he shifted the familiar wraps that made up his cushion. "Even though they may be surrounded by others much of the time, there's still a sense of detachment, of isolation. I've always had to be on guard, because when someone attempts to get close to me, I become suspicious of their motives. Everyone wants something, and if you play favorites, you run the risk of alienating the masses you're trying to lead. It's never easy."

"What's gotten you through?" I queried.

"Faith mostly," he answered. "Of course, I've had numerous conversations with God, and that helps. But these people have seen Him work as well. It's just that their memories are about as long as snake legs."

"What have you done for me lately?" I questioned as the Hebrews might have asked.

"Exactly. What have you done for me today?" he countered. "A leader has to understand human nature at its lowest common denominator and be equipped to deal with it on a daily basis. Actually, after the last sixty years, I don't think anything could surprise me. Even your arrival here wasn't much of a shock, Brad."

"I have to admit, Moses, I wouldn't have been surprised if I'd been stoned. My story seems far-fetched."

"That's just it," he said emphatically. "Part of being a good leader is not jumping to conclusions. Suppose you were lying. What did I have to fear from you? Sooner or later the truth would come out, and I could always deal with it then. Wisdom dictates that you don't take any drastic action that can wait, especially if you don't have enough information. Suppose we'd killed you and found out later you were really God's messenger. Do you know what a schmuck is?"

"I've heard the term." I grinned.

"But there's something else that's kept me on track, and

that's vision. I was devastated when we didn't go into
Canaan forty years ago, but I never gave up focusing on that
goal. Even as an old man, I still have a little fire left in my
belly. We can do this, and I believe we will. I still have it in
my heart to keep this beleaguered nation determined to
meet the challenge. Motivation—that's a big part of leadership, perhaps the greatest part."

"Did you ever seriously consider calling it quits?"

"Seriously?" he pondered aloud. "I guess the truth is,
I always knew in the back of my mind that I would see this
through, one way or another. I think that's what distin-
guishes a true leader from someone who's simply in charge.
That's not to say I never complained or asked, *Why me?* I
did that a lot. And I got angry pretty often, too. But you work
through that, and you go on."

"What was your toughest moment?" I questioned.

"I have had many trying times, but the worst by far was
returning from Mount Sinai after spending forty days receiv-
ing the law from God. I came down the mountain, exhausted
yet excited, thinking what a wonderful time we'll share as I
read what God has given us. I wanted to get some much
needed rest. And what did I see? My people, dancing
around a fire like crazed chickens, and a golden calf in the
middle of a platform. Of course, I was furious! I threw down
the tablets. They broke—and guess what? I had to go back
up the mountain and do it all over again. You know, Brad,
that was forty years ago, and it still grinds my wheat. The
icing on the manna was finding out who spearheaded making the idol."

"And it was...?"

"My brother."

We sat there quietly for a time before I spoke again.
"Would you like some wine, Moses?"

"Good thinking," he said resolutely. "Get the big cups."

*chapter
eight*

JOSHUA

I HAD BEEN AT THE HEBREW ENCAMPMENT FOR NEARLY
A MONTH AND A HALF, AND I BEGAN TO OBSERVE THOSE
AROUND ME WITH RENEWED INTEREST. ALTHOUGH MY
LIFE ESSENTIALLY CONSISTED OF TENDING SHEEP AND
GOATS AND SPENDING TIME EVERY THURSDAY WITH
MOSES, THE OTHER ISRAELITES WITH WHOM I CAME IN
CONTACT SEEMED TO BE FILLED WITH ANTICIPATION.
MORALE WAS INCREASING, EVEN AS MOSES' LIFE WAS
TRICKLING AWAY.

As promised, Joshua appeared a few days later. He
spoke briefly to my tending partners, then suggested I
accompany him to the Jordan River, a five-mile walk. On
the way, he talked only about the spring season, asking
about my experiences with herding and my relationships
with my coworkers—nothing of serious substance. When
we reached the east bank of the river, he sat down and
motioned for me to follow. A lazy breeze taunted us and
eddied the slow-moving walnut brown water just below.

"You're still a bit of mystery to us," he began. "But we're seldom surprised by what or whom God sends our way."

"I didn't plan to come here," I answered honestly. "I have no idea how long I'll be staying or how—or if—I'll be returning to my own time. I've pondered it quite a bit lately, and there's a part of me that's resolved to not knowing. Something tells me everything is okay, but I can't help being a little worried."

"Do you have a family?" he asked, echoing a concern for me that I'd yet to experience in this place. I knew it wasn't that Moses didn't care. He was focused on his own mission, his own time. I respected that beyond measure. But Joshua was charismatic, vibrant, charming; if he wasn't actually interested in me, he was one phenomenal actor.

"Yes. A wife and a married daughter," I told him, seeing their faces in my mind, "and two grandkids that defy adjectives. It's all very strange because, in a way, I feel as though I haven't left them."

"Perhaps you haven't," Joshua grinned. "Love is like that." I took solace in his words, and his candor offered assurance. "Isn't it ironic that even the man from the future is uncertain about his fate?" he quipped, smiling again.

"Moses is wise for deciding he didn't want to know the shape of things to come," I announced. "I just need to follow his example."

"Well said," Joshua affirmed. "Speaking of Moses, he seems quite impressed with you."

"Really?" I asked in amazement. "Do you think so?"

"Oh, without a doubt," he assured me. "He's taken with your interest in him and your, shall we say, *unusual* circumstances."

"It's funny, Joshua. He's asked almost nothing about me. In fact, you're the first to inquire about my family. Even my fraternal shepherds haven't asked."

"Why do you suppose that is, Brad?" he queried.

"Well, Moses determined early on that knowing the future was probably not what God had in mind, so he's avoided it. And..."Then it hit me; my chin dropped to my chest. "You've talked to Ebadiah and Idbash, haven't you?" I suddenly felt very naive.

"Let's just say we have our own methods of containment. You do pose a potential dilemma for us, and we know our people. Do you realize what a popular man you'd be if everyone knew you could tell us the future? But I agree with Moses that the promise you represent to us is worth the risk."

"Promise? Now I'm baffled again," I admitted.

"Don't overthink this, Brad. We believe that our story, and the wisdom and experience of Moses, needs to be preserved, to be carried through time. That's important to us as a nation. Since none of us know what's going to happen, you may be our best assurance on that count. Look, Moses likes you, he enjoys your visits, and he believes you sincerely want to transport our message, our *heart*, to your time in the future. We don't know how that will happen, but we're a people accustomed to miracles."

"Do you think there's one left for me?" I looked Joshua squarely in the eyes.

"God never runs out of miracles."

THURSDAYS WITH MOSES

chapter nine

THE SIXTH THURSDAY:

WE TALK ABOUT HUMAN NATURE

THE FAMILIAR SMELL OF MOSES' TENT WAS AS
WELCOME AS THE AROMA OF SPRING LILACS
AFTER A LONG WINTER, AND I WAS GREATLY
ANTICIPATING HIS RESPONSE TO MY VISIT WITH
JOSHUA. THE CONTAINMENT ISSUE WEIGHED
HEAVILY ON MY MIND, AND WHILE I WAS A BIT
EMBARRASSED ABOUT BEING DUPED, I WAS
EQUALLY CONCERNED ABOUT TRUST.

"It's Thursday already?" Moses protested upon my arrival.

"Would you like me to come back another time?" I suggested cautiously.

"No, no. It's not that," he assured me. "It just seems like when I turned a hundred and five, the calendar became a hyena, running faster and faster and laughing all the way!"

I smiled, but it was half-patronizing. Compared to my world, the lifestyle here was like watching hair grow; yet the passage of time was relative. To my elderly sage, the sundial was moving much too fast.

"Joshua and I walked to the river on Tuesday," I reported. "I finally figured out why no one's asked me any personal questions."

"You're still young and trusting," Moses rejoined. "That's a *good* thing, so please don't take this personally. I've spent the last forty-odd years with these Hebrew people. To be honest, I'm pleased that only a handful observed your arrival. We were able to quell the few rumors early on, and we knew that Idbash and Ebadiah were reliable. They're under strict orders."

"If you had told me sooner, I would have respected your wishes," I offered.

"I know that now—but what did I know of you when you arrived? Brad, my people have been little more than nomads for as long as the majority of them can remember, and the older ones were slaves prior to that. Suppose they found out you were from the future and had reliable knowledge about the results of our upcoming battles for the Promised Land? I decided early on not to ask because I've spent the last half of my life trying my best to trust God. But that goes against human nature—even my own!"

"But you hardly wavered," I countered, defending him.

"*Hardly wavering* after all I've been through is scarcely what I'd call a victory. I shouldn't have budged an inch. So if Moses, the leader, still has room to wiggle, consider what Joe Hebrew out there would do. Pretty soon you'd be mobbed by people asking, 'What will happen at Jericho?' or 'How many men will die if we attempt to take Ai?' Suppose you say you don't know? What do you think might happen? Do you think we'd be able to protect you?"

"I'm sorry," I admitted.

"Don't apologize. You've been direct and honest, and I couldn't ask for more. But let's go one step further: Do you think this nation would ever have a home if they somehow envisioned significant casualties, which are almost inevitable in the coming battles? Where would that leave us?"

"It only took a handful of men to incite the fear that kept you from taking Canaan forty years ago," I acknowledged.

"You're getting it," he concluded. "I like to think that love, kindness, and compassion are strong emotions, and they are. But fear and greed are equally powerful. Having access to information about future events appeals to both of those emotions. At times God has given me hints about certain incidents, but usually in a broad sense or only for His purposes in the short term. He knows my limitations."

"Do you think people are basically evil?" I asked, wondering if my discerning counselor would attempt such a theologically loaded question.

"People are just people," he began, without any outward sign of forethought. "Most are weak, intellectually and morally. They want to do good, but human nature is like the instinct of an animal—you fend for yourself and try to survive. Once you have enough, you might think about helping others. There are always exceptions, but that's the rule."

"So it comes down to selfishness?" I clarified.

"I think that's reasonable to say. We know what we need and what we want. We look for what's tangible that will fill the bill. What we see usually takes priority over what we can't see. Why did so many of my brothers and sisters want to return to Egypt as soon as we were tested in the desert? Their fear overcame their faith, and their stomachs dictated their responses. Is that selfish? Probably at its root, it is."

"But," I persisted, "is that necessarily evil?"

Moses hesitated. "Evil? I guess I would stop short of that. Sin? Yes, because sin simply means missing the mark—not doing your best or not doing what you know to be right. If you expect and desire a greater payoff, it may mean letting your stomach growl once in a while."

"You've witnessed all kinds of selfishness during these last forty years, haven't you?" I suggested.

"Did Noah have a big brown boat?" he responded, with a friendly twinge of sarcasm. "The world is full of folks who'll ask you to do things they'd never do themselves: They want you to work harder than they're willing to for less reward, or they want you to give more than they're willing to. You make the world better while they reap the benefits. I've encountered plenty of those. There is also an abundance of human beings who will flatten you into the dirt after you've gone out of your way to be kind to them."

He reached for his cup, brought it to his lips, and sipped carefully. "The world tends to have more takers than givers, Brad—at least it often seems that way. But you know, after all I've seen and learned in these 120 years, I know it's still best to be a giver. You must understand this before you can begin to know the heart of God."

That night I lay on the floor of my tent, staring into the unforgiving darkness above me. A pestering west wind harassed the tired fabric, snapping it in a dozen places simultaneously, as if a troop of poltergeists had selected me for their evening's mischief.

The heart of God. I played and replayed Moses' words in my head. There had been times I'd thought the selfish people of my own world had the best idea, that perhaps it made more sense to grab and hold on than to give away what you worked for, often to be unappreciated or mistreated in the bargain. Moses surely knew better, and I knew in my soul he was right.

As slowly as this ancient world turned, it still afforded me plenty to think about.

THE SEVENTH
THURSDAY:
WE TALK ABOUT POSTERITY

"I'LL BE ADDRESSING THE PEOPLE ON THE SABBATH," MOSES INFORMED ME. I MADE MYSELF AS COMFORTABLE AS ONE COULD THREE MILLENNIA PRIOR TO THE INVENTION OF THE LA-Z-BOY RECLINER. "SOME OF THESE YOUNG FOLKS WILL BE HEARING ME DO THIS FOR THE FIRST TIME, BUT," HE PAUSED, "IT WILL ALSO BE THE LAST. THE NEXT THREE SABBATHS WILL BE SET ASIDE SO THAT I CAN DO THIS RIGHT."

"Right?" I questioned.

"Absolutely," he said immovably. "There is much to tell, and my scribes will be writing. It's going to take some time. We'll arrange some relief for your tending—I'd like you to be there."

"Of course," I said. "I want to hear what you have to say. What will you be discussing?"

"Where we've come from, where we're going. The importance of following God's laws: His blessings if we do and the curses we can expect if we choose other paths. After a hundred years or so, you acquire a lot of material." The corners of his mouth curled up slightly.

"Would you like me to write some opening humor for you?" I offered, with my tongue planted firmly in my cheek.

"Thank you, but they've all heard about Adam hoping for Eve to turn over a new leaf. I think we'll keep this fairly serious. All kidding aside, Brad, I *am* concerned about this generation and those to come. It's so critical that they do this according to God's plan. When I close my eyes for the last time, I need to know that my people are committed to the Lord, to His law, to Joshua and the leaders in charge. In many ways, the years ahead will be more trying than all of this wandering."

"You've surely had tougher assignments, Moses," I said. "These are your people. They'll accept your advice." My jocular demeanor began to wane as I realized I had just been invited to Deuteronomy Live, my aging Hebrew leader's final reading of the Law and the series of speeches he would offer before his impending death. Witnessing biblical history was one thing; losing this old friend, I was certain, would be quite another.

"This discourse will be the sum and substance of my leadership, my dreams, my life. But it will be much more: who we are as a people and what God intends for us. We finally have the opportunity to establish a homeland for our children and their children and the generations to come for countless days. We can't afford to blow it."

"You certainly have to feel good about Joshua," I offered, trying to inject hope.

"That goes without saying," Moses followed. "But this is a young nation. Most of them can't conceive of how much is riding on their actions. I realize the youthful often resent the attempts of their elders to force traditional values on them, but this will be my last opportunity. I *have* to succeed."

"Is there anything I can do to help?" I asked, knowing how futile the question was.

"You've already been helpful, my friend," he said with a grandfatherly nod. I looked fully into his face and beheld a man who seemed noticeably older than the Moses I'd met less than two months earlier.

Determined, he continued. "Most people spend their lives thinking just about to the end of their noses. In fact, I'd venture that the greatest problems of humanity are caused by our failure to look down the road, to consider how the actions we take today will play out a week, six months, or ten years from now.

"But, Brad, there should come a point in a man's life when he begins to understand that the only things worth doing are those things that will outlive him. I was almost eighty when we left Egypt, so I was already thinking along those lines to a certain degree, but I also figured that if we took Canaan right away, I would have a few years left to relax and enjoy the fruits of our efforts.

"When God told me we would be wandering for the next forty years, I was angry for awhile. Although it's never left me entirely, I've put it in perspective. With each passing day, the importance of establishing a homeland for future generations occupies a greater portion of my thoughts. If no one ever remembers me, so be it. But these people are my family. They'll be the ones who'll live on. They deserve whatever I have left."

"I think their ears will be open," I assured.

"And why do you think that's so?" he questioned.

"Because you're *Moses*. Where I come from, that still means something."

Moses engaged my eyes directly, squinted, and rested his chin between his thumb and first finger. "Thank you," he said softly. "That's good to know."

As I headed back toward the east ridge to resume my role as guardian of the goats, I contemplated a thousand scenarios. To the best of my biblical recollection, Moses indeed gave three sermons to the people, which made up his last Old Testament book. Of course, one thing I remembered perfectly was the fact that God never allowed Moses to enter Canaan. He only got to view it from nearby Mount Nebo. It was his last recorded act before his death.

So Moses would die; Joshua would rally the people and head for Jericho. Where would that leave me? To be the very first American to spend his middle age and retirement years as an anonymous shepherd in the land that time forgot?

chapter eleven

THE FIRST MESSAGE

THE CAMP WAS BUZZING EARLY SATURDAY MORNING. UNLIKE MODERN TIMES, WHEN THIS MIGHT HAVE MEANT TV CARTOONS, VOCIFEROUS CHILDREN, AND A CAT AND DOG PARADE, THIS SETTLEMENT WAS ALIVE WITH FESTIVE ANTICIPATION AS WELL AS WHAT I PERCEIVED TO BE GENUINE CONCERN. THIS WAS THE SABBATH—A FAR CRY FROM ANY HAVEN FOR THE WEEKEND WARRIORS OF MY TIME.

The day itself was blueprint-perfect: windless, just warm enough, with less than a handful of pebbly clouds already melting into a powder blue sky. Apparently God was no longer miffed at Moses.

I arrived at his tent early, after a man probably not yet twenty years old came to assume my watch. Although these folks were generally careful about working on the Sabbath, you simply could not trust a couple thousand sheep and goats to stay out of trouble. This lad would get his opportunity to rest later.

"Looks like God's on your side today, Moses," I proclaimed enthusiastically as he exited the tent.

"Good morning," he said rather precisely, as if reading from a script. "We'll be doing this at the west base of Mount Nebo. The sound carries well there. I'd like you to sit near the front, but off to one side. Try to be as inconspicuous as you can. We want to avoid distractions."

I suddenly thought of Jack Lord as Steve McGarrett, firing a salvo of commands to Dano and the boys. Moses was in a zone, wholly focused on the task before him, and I wasn't about to tamper with his psyche. "I understand," I said dutifully. "I'll do whatever you ask."

Before he could respond, Joshua appeared. Smiling and self-assured, his presence was an ineffable comfort. "God is with us, my friends. What a great and memorable day this will be," he announced, temporarily breaking the spell Moses had cast upon himself.

"Memorable is what I'm hoping for," admitted Moses.

The sheer number of Israelites gathered at the mountain's base reminded me of the pictures of Yasgur's Farm in 1969, but I was certain this crowd numbered far more. Counting was out of the question. I wondered how everyone would be able to hear Moses. There were no giant speaker columns or 10,000-watt public-address systems. "The sound carries well," he had told me, but I knew enough about acoustics to know it would be impossible for his aging voice to penetrate the ears of anyone more than a few yards away.

Evidently, these outings had taught the Israelites some audio fundamentals. As blocks of people took their places, relay men holding crude megaphones positioned themselves in front of each group. I had to smile. Although this was going to take awhile, I couldn't help admiring their tenacity and ingenuity.

Moses stood, and the multitudes rose to their feet, applauding, shouting, and blessing God. Some had brought tambourines and shook them jubilantly. Could this assembled nation really be the descendants of the grumpy, whining Hebrews whom Moses had tolerated for the last four decades?

The noise increased to a fever pitch when Joshua joined him on the mountain stage. Several minutes passed, and the pair seemed to be graciously basking in the moment. It was as close as Moses would get to a retirement party.

He raised his arms to quiet the crowd. "Forty long years ago," he began, "God told us to leave Mount Sinai and to take possession of Canaan, the land He had promised to our fathers, Abraham, Isaac, and Jacob. When we drew near to it, we agreed to send in twelve spies, one from each tribe, to investigate. Although two of our men returned declaring that with God's help, we could surely defeat the inhabitants there, others lacked faith, some even saying that the Lord hated us and brought us out of Egypt to die at the hands of the Amorites.

"Because of this, God grew angry and promised that none of those vile men would ever live to see us claim our homeland. He found favor only with Joshua and Caleb, who are still with us today. During these last years, although we have seen much strife, our Lord has not abandoned us. We have witnessed His intervention on many occasions. And finally, here we stand, at the dawn of a new opportunity to fulfill God's desire, which is one with our own. This time, we must not fail.

"If we are to ensure victory, we must be careful not to repeat our mistakes, and the greatest of these is failure to trust our God. If we trust Him, we must work hard to keep the laws He gave us at Mount Sinai. Please hear me, O children of Israel, as I repeat the words of the Lord: 'I am the God who delivered you out of Egyptian slavery, and I shall be your only Lord.

" 'See to it that you avoid idols. They have no power. I am able to show mercy to whom I please, especially to those who love Me and obey My instructions. Bow only to Me.

" 'Do not take My name in vain.

" 'Keep the Sabbath Day holy. It is a day for you and your household to rest and remember Me.

" 'If you want to live a long and prosperous life in the Promised Land, treat your father and mother with respect.

" 'Do not murder.

" 'Live a life that is free of sexual sin.

" 'Do not steal.

" 'Always tell the truth.

" 'Don't be envious of anything that belongs to your neighbor.'

"These are the rules that your heavenly Father has ordered for those who will be called by His name. Descendants of Abraham, are you willing to live by these laws?"

The roar of response began from the front rows, growing

to deafening proportions as the callers repeated Moses' question to their respective throngs. They rose to their feet, creating a sweeping effect as they stood. This was far better than any wave I had seen in Tiger Stadium.

As the masses quieted once again, Moses began a discourse on how the people should conduct themselves in the new land. My thoughts were still fixed on what he had just shared. Of course, it was merely a retelling of the Ten Commandments, but the ideas struck me with a certain newness, and my mind began to race like a spooked Secretariat.

These were the rules that continued to cause controversy in twenty-first-century America, and cases were ongoing regarding which walls were legal for their posting. I knew there were no easy answers, but hearing this from Moses just east of the Jordan only seemed to raise more questions. I grasped his plea for allegiance to God, avoiding idols, honesty, and respect for parents. It was difficult to argue with any of these. But there were problems.

Working on Saturday could get a person stoned—*real* stones thudding angrily against real flesh, until the battered, bloodied offender breathed his last. Yes, the body and soul need rest—my world of the future should recognize that, too—but this was a cogent example of harsh Old Testament justice. (I could only assume stonings happened rarely. How could people witness such a scene without having it Velcro itself to their minds forever?) *Habitual criminal* was not part of the Hebrew vocabulary.

The words *sexual sin* rattled in my brain like an old jalopy. This culture still considered women to be chattel, and while that didn't necessarily mean men didn't love their wives, it did suggest that expectations were much different than where I came from. Those adjunct female partners affectionately known as concubines were standard fare. Women had few options, and there was no legislation pending to alter the system.

The final conundrum was murder. "Thou shalt not kill," King James's translators had penned in the seventeenth century, and every baby boomer in America who ever attended Sunday school knew that version. Later, many of them found themselves in jungles, killing and being killed.

I knew this could be problematic for Moses since his armies would seemingly be defying this law in order to vanquish the current residents of Canaan. But he saw in the command a different purpose. "Thou shalt not kill," at this juncture in time, was about homicide, Hebrews killing Hebrews—nothing more. To the Israelites this was war, and for better or worse, war always redefines the rules.

Envy seemed a strange child to place at the end of the line, and it sat uncomfortably on my lap. Having arrived just a few short weeks ago, the wonder of meeting Moses and Joshua, witnessing biblical history—the encompassing awe of my situation—had overshadowed my thinking more than I'd realized.

For some reason I'd usually thought of envy as a hallmark of the twentieth century. Who in their right mind would lose any sleep over the fact that their neighbor had a few more goats than they do or that their neighbor's camel had two humps instead of one? It seemed to me that if it isn't the Hearst Mansion or a Lamborghini, why worry about it? Anyway, isn't it all about the American dream: a nice house, two cars, a boat, two kids, and a cocker spaniel? (And people could say all that in the same breath!)

Moses had no knowledge of Tudor houses or sports cars. He simply understood the hearts of human beings, where an envy gene has existed forever.

I had been lost in my thoughts for some time, and my surroundings had taken on a surreal appearance. Refocusing, I listened as Moses concluded his comments.

"Remember, if you prosper, it will only be because God has allowed it and blessed you. If you try to claim the credit and forget about Him, you will fall. God is your strength. God is your salvation. Write this in your hearts. Carry it with you always."

Joshua immediately stood, and the masses followed his lead. Again came the applause and the tambourines. Moses raised his aging arms in gratitude one last time and descended slowly down the mountain's gently sloping foot, disappearing far quicker than his congregation wished.

I watched his frame become smaller, smaller, then disappear, but I did not follow him. He would need to rest and hadn't requested that I visit. Our day was Thursday. It appeared there would be no shortage of things to talk about.

THURSDAYS WITH MOSES

chapter twelve

THE EIGHTH
THURSDAY:

WE TALK ABOUT THE JOURNEY

MY EXCURSIONS ON THE INCREASINGLY FAMILIAR PATH TO MOSES' TENT RARELY PRESENTED ME WITH OPPORTUNITIES TO INTERACT WITH STRANGERS. TODAY WAS AN EXCEPTION. I HAD WALKED BUT A FEW HUNDRED YARDS THROUGH THE WELL-PACKED SAND WHEN SHE SURREPTITIOUSLY APPEARED BY MY SIDE, WITH A "SHALOM, TRAVELER!" THAT RATTLED ME TO ATTENTION LIKE HEARING A POLICE SIREN. I FLINCHED, AND HER LAUGHTER SOUNDED LIKE A MISCHIEVOUS GIRL AMBUSHING HER FATHER WITH A SUPER SOAKER. EMBARRASSED BUT RELIEVED TO HAVE SOME SPIRITED COMPANY, I LET DOWN MY GUARD AND OFFERED MY BEST OKAY-YOU-GOT-ME SMILE.

"How did you get so close without my seeing you?" I asked, realizing she couldn't be much more than twenty and had gotten the drop on me.

"I'm magic," she teased. Her dark eyes danced in an angel's face with a demon's smile. "Surely you know about magic!"

"Isn't that a bit risky around here?" I queried, knowing the law called for the killing of witches.

"Just like everything else. Do you know *you* could get trampled in a goat stampede—and you'd be just as dead as someone those superstitious people executed for doing something they didn't understand."

I looked carefully at her. This was a young woman who had arrived at some thoughtful albeit dangerous conclusions. "A goat stampede, eh?" I smiled. "How did you know I was tending the goats?"

"Well, first of all," she pointed out, "there's hardly anything but sheep and goats in the direction you're coming from, so it's likely you've been leaning on a shepherd's crook. It's also pretty obvious that you don't belong here. You could stay in this Ammon sun naked for the rest of your life and never get your skin the right color."

Her tone became a bit more serious. "In case you're interested, I don't belong here either, but for different reasons than you."

"What's your name?" I asked, deciding I had nothing to lose. She hesitated.

"You can call me Eve."

"Ah, so you're first among women!"

"Oooh, I like that," she replied. "And your name?"

"You don't already know? There's actually a void in your omniscience?"

"Tell me!" she insisted.

"Okay, call me Adam," I responded, feeling superior.

"No way! You're twice my age. Adam was young and gorgeous."

"He was also mature—and semicute," I informed her. "After that he became very old, and then ancient. But that still wasn't the end of it. By the time he died, he was 930 years old. Tell me, Evie, have you ever seen a gorgeous 930 year old?"

"Does middle age make *everyone* this testy?" she taunted.

"Pretty much. And I bet *you* were a lot cuter when you were two or three."

"Enjoy your visit with Moses, Adam," she said with a laugh, dropping back. "I'll see you again."

"Thanks! Wait a minute! How did you know where I—" I turned, but there was no Eve.

By the time I reached my destination, I wondered if the meeting had really happened. The heat of the day leaned on me like a debt collector, and I questioned if the desert and the whole of this experience had finally rendered me psychotic. "Perhaps any man who finds himself lost three thousand years in the past should begin by diagnosing his own sanity," I said aloud to no one. But Moses *was* real. Of this, I was certain.

As I straightened myself after bending slightly to enter his tent, Moses immediately embraced me, and I was at once thankful and dumbfounded. This had never happened before. I sensed he was growing aware that our remaining hours together were limited. He seemed thinner and smelled musty, like a damp Michigan basement after an August rain. Amid the heat and livestock, few of these folks carried a bubble-bath aroma. Surprisingly, my olfactory sense had adapted quickly. This smell was different though. It was familiar but not associated with good memories.

"Your presentation last Sabbath was amazing," I said, eager

to focus on something positive. "The people loved you."

"It's one thing to love someone; it's entirely different to obey them," he countered. "Love can be an emotional thing—as tenuous as getting caught up in the moment. But obedience is a day-to-day exercise. It's work, and it takes more discipline than many of these people have. They think they've been tested, but most of those who were put through their paces died over these last forty years. They couldn't cut it. Some of that Sabbath crowd will be joining them soon enough."

"But won't God protect you? Where does He fit into all of this?" I asked.

"Oh, He'll be around, rest assured," Moses answered. "But this is a new chapter, a new journey. Joshua will certainly face all of the challenges I've experienced—and more. For all intents and purposes, he has a fresh, enthusiastic nation with a new plan. I pray that they're beginning to understand where their fathers erred and are resolved not to make the same mistakes—although human nature being what it is, some mistakes, probably *most* of them, are bound to be repeated."

"Then it's a pilgrimage of individuals rather than a Hebrew journey?"

"In many ways, yes. Consider how one person's success or happiness can affect others in a similar, positive way. Then contrast that with how fear, greed, envy—those negative habits—influence our neighbors. Everyone's life is a journey, much like the experience of my people. We originally came to Egypt to escape a famine, and for a long time, we prospered. Then along came a leader who feared our potential because there were so many of us, so he managed to reduce us to slaves.

"Men have always gone where they could be best fed.

I'd guess self-preservation is still popular in your time as well. If you're not careful, if you stop looking ahead, you can find yourself in a situation that's worse than being hungry. Then you have to decide what you're willing to risk just to get back to square one."

"So you're going in circles," I inserted.

He seemed to ignore me. "At some point, you either grow up or die. You decide that you're living far below your potential, and it becomes a defining moment. You either succumb to mediocrity, or you make up your mind to set yourself free."

"Grow up or die?" I repeated. "That's pretty harsh."

"Not really," Moses countered. "Think, Brad. Fear and greed are two powerful emotions. I like to consider myself an optimist, but I'm honest about the impact of these feelings. Most everyone fears death because it represents the unknown. So how many people are willing to risk what they have, even if it's somewhat meager, to possibly end up with nothing? As you can see, greed naturally applies here as well, although we usually think of it in terms of wealth. But what about greed for life? Without life, wealth means nothing.

"We took a great leap of faith when we left Egypt, even though there were plenty of miracles to inspire us. But it was only a year or so later that we lost our faith, our nerve, our identity. When you're little more than reluctant nomads for half a lifetime, you're overdue for an evaluation. This is ours."

Moses sat quietly for several minutes. I said nothing. When the silence became too much for me, I asked, "Are you going to rally the troops again this Sabbath?"

"Yes," he said. "I'll make certain we send someone again to cover your tending duties. Go in peace. I'll see you then."

chapter thirteen

THE PLAN

MOST OF MY DAYS TENDING THE LIVESTOCK WERE NOW SPENT IN CONTEMPLATION AND DOING MY BEST TO RECONSTRUCT MOSES' EXACT WORDS ON MY LEGAL PAD. I'D TAKEN COPIOUS NOTES AND WAS AIMING FOR PERFECTION. I NOTICED I WAS DOWN TO THE LAST TEN SHEETS OF UNUSED PAPER, WHEN THE WORD "PREDESTINATION" PROJECTED ITSELF ON THE BIG SCREEN OF MY MIND. THERE WOULD BE ONE MORE SERMON FROM MOSES AFTER TOMORROW, AND IF FATE COOPERATED, MAYBE THREE OR FOUR MORE THURSDAY INTERVIEWS. I HADN'T WRITTEN ON THE BACKS OF THE PAPER, AND THAT WOULD BE MY CONTINGENCY PLAN. YET THE PERSISTENT KNOT IN MY CEREBRAL CORTEX TORMENTED ME WITH THE POSSIBILITY THAT IT WOULDN'T BE NECESSARY. A VOICE EMANATING FROM MY SPIRIT SEEMED TO SAY THAT TEN SHEETS WOULD BE ENOUGH.

I had too much time to think. Fortunately, the heat of the day and the walking were typically enough to tire me physically so that I could fall asleep at night. My mental stamina was suspect. I knew I would soon lose Moses. Joshua was a friend, but he had other concerns on his mind with the coming assault on Canaan and his immediate leadership duties.

Would I be expected to fight with the army? Would I have any chance to return home after Moses helped me fill the last ten pages of my tablet? Should I begin looking for the Urim and Thummim, hoping they could reverse whatever part they might have played in my untimely disposition?

Then there was the mystery of Eve. She'd said she didn't belong here either. What did she know? Could she help me? Would I put myself in danger by associating with her?

I needed a plan, and I finally formulated one. I would focus on my immediate purpose. I would continue to record the wisdom of Moses and see the project through to the end. Then I'd discuss my fate with Joshua. If he offered no hope, I would find the Urim and Thummim, even if it meant risking my present safety. My friendship with Joshua should get me close enough to the artifacts that I could possibly even "borrow" them if necessary. I would try to find Eve only as a last resort. This plan seemed like my best course of action. It offered me three possibilities—maybe all long shots, but it beat the alternative. Now that it was settled in my head, I was once again ready to complete the task at hand: sitting at the feet of my aging mentor and harvesting his wisdom.

I awoke Saturday morning with a renewed appreciation for where I was and what I was witnessing. I reminded myself that I was living a Jules Verne dream, the wishful thinking of millions of romantics since the idea of time travel first popped into a human mind. No amount of money could buy this experience. For once in my life I was unique, special, chosen.

chapter fourteen

THE BACK WAY
TO NEBO:
FROM THE MOUTHS OF CAVES

THE SUN HAD YET TO PEER OVER THE RIDGE WHEN MY SUBSTITUTE TENDER ARRIVED, A STURDY, SERIOUS-LOOKING YOUNG MAN NAMED SALAH. "JOSHUA HAS SENT ME TO TEND IN YOUR STEAD," HE SAID, AS IF REPORTING TO A SENIOR OFFICER. "THEY ARE EXPECTING YOU AT THE GATHERING OF ISRAEL, AT THE FOOT OF NEBO."

"Thank you," I offered. "Idbash is at the north watch."

"God bless you, sir," he added. I turned back and gave him a fatherly wink, and he succumbed to an awkward smile. It was a fairly good start to my day, but events were about to become far more interesting.

The path leading to Nebo would be a new one for me, and I would be traveling it alone. Moses had not asked me to meet at his tent this time, and he rightly assumed I could take this more direct route. It was a footpath that offered fresh scenery, including the mouths of a handful of mountain caves. Idbash had told me what to watch out for, including the usual snakes and scorpions. I carried a large staff, which was adequate for keeping the pests at a safe distance. I set out feeling adventurous, whistling "The Lion Sleeps Tonight."

Two caves, a twist here, a turn there, three lazy golden scorpions on a primordial gray rock catching the rays of a morning, tangerine sun, a scraggly and withered bush—this was ancient Ammon. I wondered if the picture would look much different in my time. I doubted it.

I was walking at a brisk pace (more because it felt good than due to any fears of not arriving on time) when a loud snap off to my left stole my attention. My fellow tenders had mentioned rumors of lion sightings in the past, and although rare and unconfirmed, they didn't discount them. It's amazing how quickly the mind conjures the worst possible scenarios.

"*Psssst.*"

A snake? I surveyed the area quickly and discreetly but saw no reptile. I knew I should just stay on the path and get to Nebo, but I couldn't help being curious. I took a few short, calculated steps in the direction of the sound.

"*Psssssst.*" I jumped. It was louder, closer. Looking through the scrub brush, I could see the opening of another cave. It had to be thirty yards away. I couldn't believe any snake could generate that much volume. The sunlight was pouring into the area, and the blackness just inside the opening created a stark contrast. I moved closer and heard nothing. Gripping my staff tightly with both hands, I drew the short end above my right shoulder and raised the other end waist high. I was ready for the unexpected. The cave opening was no more than ten feet in front of me.

Get out of here! my practical, conservative left brain screamed as loudly as it could, but I refused to obey. I moved carefully, methodically, to the edge of the opening.

"Eeyyyyahhhh!" A figure sprung from the darkness toward me, and in that instant I wondered if I would be killed by a beast or die of pure, unadulterated fear. I impulsively raised the staff and then stopped. It was Eve.

"Why, you little—!" I screamed, straining every atom of my better nature to avoid shouting one of the numerous epithets dying to be released from my brain. "You malicious little—!" I sunk to the ground, shaking like a collie that had just crawled out of a pond, and Eve joined me there, rolling in maniacal laughter. I had made her day, quite possibly her year.

"Get it all out of your system, Adam," she said between guffaws. "I'm a malicious little *what*?"

As my parasympathetic nervous system kicked in to slow my heart rate and Eve's frenzied chortle slowly subsided, I studied her face. She somehow looked very familiar—beyond our chance meeting on the path to Moses' tent. I was almost certain I should know her. Where? How? I couldn't quite make the connection.

"The things you see when you don't have a camcorder!" she taunted. "I don't think I've ever seen anyone jump like that! Adam, this was far more cathartic than a two-hundred-dollar session with my therapist."

Camcorder? Therapist? Eve didn't belong here! Uncertain whether she was intentionally dropping broad clues or had merely let down her guard by accident, I pretended not to pay any attention.

"You were about two seconds away from becoming Eve on a stick," I assailed.

"Adam, you are an absolute riot," Eve offered through a waning chuckle. "I haven't laughed like that in years. I'd have to say that we're even now—that look of sheer terror on your face was a classic I won't forget!"

"We're even? What do you mean by that? What did I ever do to you?"

"I have something to show you, Adam," she offered. "That is, if you don't mind stepping into this cave that just took ten years off your life. I guess that would make you somewhere near Moses' age now, huh?"

"I'm still holding this staff, sweetie," I responded, "and my patience is no match for Job. You have a couple of thugs in there who want my sunglasses or something?"

"Oh, c'mon," she teased. "Your curiosity got you there once, and you're still alive. I promise, no pranks this time."

"And I'm supposed to just keep playing Mr. Naive for all of your tricks?"

"I have something that might end up in a museum someday," she said.

Museum! I stared at her winsome face with a different kind of shock. She reached out for my hand and when I grasped hers, it hit me like the stone that dropped Goliath: *Eve was the lady at the Eretz!*

"I bumped into you at the museum in Israel," I said, almost apologetically.

"Is that what you call it?" she asked, suddenly letting go of my hand. "In hockey I think they refer to it as checking."

"Oh, please! I barely nudged you."

"You nearly knocked me over!" she argued. "I've never seen anyone so excited over a couple of artifacts."

"Seriously? I pushed you that hard?"

"Yes, you did. But you've paid a price. Like I said, we're even."

"Wow, I can't imagine what I would've suffered if I'd actually hurt you!"

Eve laughed again. "I grew up with six brothers, and I was pushed and shoved a lot, but I learned ways to defend myself. I guess I haven't lost my touch."

"I feel sorry for your brothers," I said, nursing my ego. "But I apologize for what happened at the museum. I guess I didn't realize how captivated I was with the Urim and Thummim. I mean it. I'm sorry."

"I like you, Adam," she responded, "and you're forgiven. I have a feeling we're going to need each other if we're ever going to get back. Come with me."

She reached down and took my hand once again. While this baffled me a little, I knew she was right. We would probably be better off working together, and if this was her way of demonstrating trust, so be it. Once at the entrance, she led me inside.

We were out of the sun's direct light but not so far inside the grotto that we couldn't see. Just a few steps in and two or three to the right, she stopped, bent down, and picked up a small crock stuffed full of cloth. Handing it to me, she said, "Unwrap this carefully. We don't need another calamity."

My heart was racing again. When I unrolled the fabric, I was speechless. It was the Urim.

"H...how did you get this?" I stammered, after my brain started firing on all eight cylinders.

"I've been here as long as you have, Adam. Whatever you did back there at the Eretz brought at least the two of us here. I've had some time on my hands, and I've spent most of it trying to get to the artifacts. I figured it was the only chance I'd have of getting back."

"Do you have the mate to this?"

"I plan to. Right now, no one knows this is missing. From what I've been able to learn, they'll be using both of them for some sort of ceremony next month. I almost had the Thummim, but a priest showed up, and I was nearly caught. I brought this here for safekeeping. If anyone finds out, I'm history."

"Isn't that what we already are?" I couldn't resist the bad pun, but Eve was right, and my imagination might be taxed to envision the penalty for stealing a Hebrew oracle of this significance. Such a punishment would obviously end in death, but I had a feeling death itself might be the easy part.

"You're putting a lot of trust in me, Eve. I certainly can't promise you that either of us will ever get back. This whole thing defies logic. We're living science fiction here."

"Don't think I don't know that," she said. "Just promise me that you'll do what you can, that you won't try to leave without me, and that you'll keep your eyes and ears open. Let's try to help each other get back alive."

"You don't have a DeLorean hidden in this cave, do you?" I teased, attempting to check her sudden sobriety.

"Sorry, Marty." Eve smiled, but it was a worried smile.

"I promise," I said. "We're officially in this together." I

wrapped the cloth around the Urim, placed it carefully in the crock, and handed it back to her. She lightly placed it back on the floor of the cave, and we made our way out.

"I've got to get to Mount Nebo," I said. "Moses is speaking again today."

"So I hear," she answered. Eve turned and looked at me, then extended her right hand toward me. I stepped forward and clasped her hand within both of mine. "Friends?" she queried.

"Friends," I pledged. "Eve, we'll find a way back somehow. And when we do, we'll celebrate three thousand years of friendship. If that doesn't make the Guinness world records, nothing will."

"Get to Nebo, Adam," she said, resigned.

"Where can I find you?" I asked.

"Better that I find you," she advised. "I know where you live."

"Eve always had the jump on Adam," I admitted.

"It's a woman's role," she countered.

I winked and turned to leave. I would never get the last word on this young lady. A quick-thinking ally could only be a plus for me here, and now it appeared that I had one.

chapter fifteen

THE SECOND MESSAGE

I WAS BACK ON THE PATH, NOW SOMEWHAT CON-
CERNED ABOUT ARRIVING ON TIME FOR MOSES' SER-
MON. THE LAST THING I NEEDED WAS TO HAVE TO
FABRICATE AN EXCUSE FOR BEING LATE. FORTUN-
ATELY, NO ONE HERE WORE A WATCH—WHICH WAS
LIBERATING IN ITS OWN OLD TESTAMENT WAY.
THERE WERE ALWAYS STRAGGLERS. IT JUST WASN'T
GOOD FOR ME TO BE AMONG THEM.

I picked up the pace, commanding my on-a-mission gait
through the exquisite desolation surrounding this foot trail
to the mountainside. I thought of Eve and the precarious
position she had placed herself in. I was sorry that my ignorance about the handling of the oracles had brought her
here, yet I couldn't help feeling good about having someone from my own time for company. Eve was no fool. Her
odds for finding a way out of this were better than my own.

Up ahead, I saw the crowds nearing the site of the
morning's homily. In a few short minutes, I succeeded in

arriving at my spot without being noticed. I sat down on a rock, gazed up into the fateful Ammon sky, and breathed a long sigh of relief.

As it turned out, I was plenty early. The throngs settled after a short time, but it seemed like an eternity before Moses arrived. I was becoming worried that he might be ill or that he had suffered some misfortune. He had been among the first on the scene for the previous outing, always prepared, always thinking, never wanting to be outfoxed by challenges or unexpected situations. The ocean of people, supposedly accustomed to life in the slow lane, was becoming noticeably restless. Even the desert sky, which earlier was on the edge of indigo, was succumbing to a wary overcast.

When the old general finally rose, a chorus of tens of thousands of Hebrew voices, from children to the aged, rolled across the natural amphitheater of Mount Nebo like a timpani crescendo. I found myself standing and shouting as if my own salvation hung in the balance, celebrating Israel, and accepting that this beleaguered nation of wanderers somehow owned a slice of my soul. Whatever plans God had previously made for this day, He'd cancelled. He was here.

Moses slowly raised his arms above his head as an act of gratitude, then waved his hands to silence the crowd. He began with all the vocal strength he could muster, noticeably less than he'd summoned just a week ago. Those 120-year-old vocal cords were sounding their age.

"You have waited here for me this morning much longer than you had expected. You were impatient and uneasy in just this child's handful of time. Our God has waited for us these last forty years—waited for us to trust in His goodness, waited for us to let Him lead us. How great is the patience of our Lord in waiting for a faithless generation to pass!

"God led your fathers and me with a cloud by day and fire by night. He will surely lead us again. Let us be careful to obey Him—and only Him—lest His fire consume us."

Moses' tardiness had been part of the strategy, and my worry about him unnecessary. But by no means had his intended effect been lost on me or those whom I was close enough to observe. We had waited no more than an hour for our keynote speaker and were growing impatient. God, on the other hand, had waited four decades.

"One week ago," he continued, "I repeated the commandments that God gave me on the holy mountain. Make sure you have written them on the tablets of your hearts. Teach them to your children: Ponder them as you walk on the paths, discuss them in your homes, post them on your gates. Think of them when you first wake in the morning and consider them before you fall asleep at night.

"Love the Lord with every ounce of your being. Follow Him with all of the strength He provides you, and it shall go well with you. Soon you will be given lands you have not worked for—amazing, great cities you had no hand in building—houses full of wonderful things you did not earn, trees and vineyards you did not plant.

"Be very careful, my children, because that is when you will be tempted to forget that it was the hand of God which provided these things. It will be then that some may say, 'Look what we have done. Look what we have accomplished by our own doing.' If you fall into that snare of pride, beware; for at that moment God may turn His face away from you and curse you.

"When God sends you across the river, you must fully conquer the nations you encounter. Do not make any compromises with them. Do not let your sons marry their daughters nor permit your daughters to wed their sons. If you do, they may tempt you to serve other gods, and if you yield to that temptation, the Lord will surely destroy you.

"Therefore, destroy the altars of the foreign gods, burn the wooden images, and knock down their sacred pillars. Remember that you are a people God has called to Himself. You are holy because He has chosen you. He has set you apart from all other races as a treasure for Himself."

Moses paused. I expected cheers and revelry, but the multitudes were nearly death silent. They were contemplating this, and I couldn't blame them—I wasn't sure how *I* would respond to being referred to as part of God's special treasure, but it was a profound image.

I pictured the coming battles—Jericho's walls falling, the initial defeat and testing of Joshua at Ai. Images of tall, intricately engraved wooden idols, possibly some covered in silver or gold. In a weak moment, anyone might be tempted to falter. Moses was asking a lot from these people, yet he recognized the alternative.

"God didn't choose us because we were the greatest of nations; indeed, we were the least. But because God made a solemn promise to your fathers, He rescued you from Egypt with His sturdy hand, honoring His word, and allowing you to walk away as Pharaoh watched in defeat.

"Therefore, understand that our God *is* God, faithful to a thousand generations of those who love and obey Him.

Those who abhor Him, He will certainly destroy; but those who love Him will be blessed with ceaseless bounty."

Moses offered no waffle room: love God and live or disobey and die. His clarity and simplicity made the choice a no-brainer. If I had a dollar for every time I'd tired of making decisions, I could treat Eve to hot goose liver and onions with dates at Kapot Tmarim—if we ever made it back to Tel Aviv. It was too bad I couldn't bring Moses with me to help me cut through all the underbrush and overhanging vines surrounding life's dilemmas. But this was his time and place. It could be no other way.

"Remember that the Lord still renders miraculous works. Consider the manna that we ate and the water that flowed from the rock at Horeb. And God has preserved your feet and your garments these last forty years."

I'd always wondered about these things. To be completely honest, I'd become skeptical about miracles as I'd grown older, and I assumed I wasn't alone. The stories were great for kids, but would any logical, thinking adult take them literally? Here was Moses, alluding to events that could have been quickly and easily disputed by some members of this audience, had there been reasonable doubt of their occurrence.

Examining the garments I had on, I found no signs of wear. Given that I'd worn them daily for more than a couple of months now, they should have admitted to some erosion, but none was visible. (I smiled when I thought of underwear I had owned for ten years, facetiously sparring with my wife when she threatened to pitch them into the trash. Of course, they looked like they'd been worn a thousand times.) And I hadn't noticed anyone here hobbling either. I would have to give Moses the benefit of the doubt.

"So walk in the ways of your Lord," he continued. "Accept the discipline He disburses, for it is just. He is bringing you into a paradise, a land of flowing fountains and rich, fertile valleys. Here you shall have everything you need and more, from pomegranates and figs to olive oil and honey. In the hills you will find copper and iron.

"But again I warn you: When you are counting your gold and your herds are too large to number, when you are fat from eating the fruits of the Promised Land, do not forget it was the guiding hand of Almighty God that brought it to pass. The hand that opens to you most surely has the power to close its fingertips tightly into its palm and bring you again to ruin."

Moses turned and walked slowly yet deliberately off the rocky rostrum. There was no applause, no shouting, no tambourines; and that was just what Moses had intended. This nation, with everything on the line, needed to ponder the consequences of misjudging a no-nonsense leader. In their case, the leader wasn't Moses. It was God.

*chapter
sixteen*

THE NINTH
THURSDAY:

WE TALK ABOUT ARRIVING

MOSES SEEMED SURPRISINGLY AT PEACE WHEN I
ARRIVED AT HIS TENT FIVE DAYS LATER. ONCE
AGAIN, HE WELCOMED ME WITH A FATHER'S
EMBRACE, AND IT STRUCK ME PROFOUNDLY THAT
OUR RELATIONSHIP WOULD NOT—COULD NOT—
BE DUPLICATED: A MENTOR WHO IS THREE THOU-
SAND YEARS SENIOR TO HIS STUDENT, AND A STU-
DENT WHO KNOWS INFORMATION HIS TEACHER
WOULD NEVER KNOW. I REALIZED ALSO THAT I
DEEPLY LOVED THIS MAN, AND IT SEEMED THAT
HE HAD, IN A STRANGE WAY, ADOPTED ME AS A
SON, A SON WHOM HE WOULD ONLY KNOW FOR
THE LAST WEEKS OF HIS LIFE.

"The ways of the Lord are often strange to men," he
offered as I settled into my familiar groundling's throne,
"and the words God gives His leaders to speak often defy

the common man's understanding."

"If you're talking about your sermon last Sabbath," I responded, "I followed you completely. It was thoughtful and effective, not to mention creative."

"Thank you. You're an uncommon man, Brad."

"Maybe. But I've heard a lot of presentations. I think you really *had* to do it this way. You had to interrupt the celebration with a heavy dose of reality. I was impressed with your honesty. In the future, we call it *tough love*."

"Tough love? I guess that does sum it up well. They need to think on this for a few days. Next week is the final speech."

"A celebration?" I queried.

"You'll be there," he stated. "I have one more shot, if this old voice holds out. With God's help, I'll have them ready to cross the Jordan."

"Milk and honey," I suggested.

"That's a metaphor," he advised. "On the other side of that river is a potential paradise for my people. If they win the battles, most everything will be theirs for the taking. Consider, Brad, leading a nation into a place where great cities are already built, houses with food prepared on the table, cattle in the barns, vineyards ripe with grapes—more than we could need or want.

"But we have two problems. First, we have to defeat the armies and those who will try to deter our mission. When I think back on what happened forty years ago, I can't help but feel there's a chance that fear could set in, and a small loss of life could lead to great discouragement. Then a few doomsayers start rattling, and we're back to the beginning. That's not my greatest concern, though."

"Really?"

"Not by a long shot," Moses said. "Do you recall how I closed my message last Sabbath?"

"Fat and sassy?" I asked.

"I didn't think I came across that way," he said.

"Not *you*, Moses! I meant that the people would become fat and sassy after they arrived in Canaan."

Moses grinned. He was still toying with me at 120 years of age. "Glad you got that. I hoped the whole morning wasn't wasted.

"Brad, God always said we are a stiff-necked people, and I suppose we have as much pride as any tribe that's walked the earth; but we're humans, and most humans have a tendency to pat themselves on the back, to take the credit, to want a little attention. I've even been guilty of that once or twice myself.

"It goes doubly so with the people, and therein lies the greater problem. I don't think conquering the land will be as potentially threatening to this nation as what could easily happen after they've taken control. I simply had to give them these last few days to take that to heart. Frankly, at some point, it's almost bound to be part of our next significant downfall."

"How long can one message hold them?" I asked.

"Only God knows," he replied. "I'm just one man who's trying to anticipate all the snares this generation might face and to prepare them as best I can. I'll be gone when they arrive."

"Arriving," I said. "I've never thought of it literally before."

Moses picked up on my tone and looked at me inquisitively.

"Moses," I said, "in my day we talk about arriving as having achieved success, usually in financial terms. It's that point when someone gets everything they've worked for, what they thought they wanted. Then they can relax and be happy from there on out. What's surprising, though, is when most people I've known have reached that pinnacle, they find it's only satisfying for a short time. Then they have to deal with the disappointment that arriving didn't equal happiness."

"Precisely," said Moses. "Now consider the fact that if my people manage a successful military campaign, they'll never have to labor for what they'll inherit. At least with the people you're talking about, they've actually invested time and effort to achieve their successes.

"In our case, our armies will fight, and everyone else will reap the benefits. Everything *just for the taking*. It would probably be much better if we could conquer the land and then keep the people occupied with building cities and houses for the next forty years. It's almost too easy."

"To arrive, all they have to do is show up." I summed.

"May God help us," Moses said.

Moses had once again piqued my wonder-worn intellect, and I contemplated his words and worries as I walked the sun-scorched dirt of Ammon to my shepherd's post. I felt I was as close as I would ever get to discovering the meaning of life—experiencing an Old Testament epiphany that could not be restrained by time.

The joy is in the building, in the work, in the doing, in the implementation of the plan. What comes after holds potential danger, at least the realistic danger of the people becoming arrogant, proud, godless. Could there be happiness in that? I doubted if it could offer any lasting satisfaction. "All things that are, are with more spirit chased than enjoyed," a Shakespearean character once observed. Moses had never authored a play, but he was familiar with his cast.

THE FINAL
MESSAGE

I IT WAS FRIDAY AFTERNOON, AND I HAD SPENT
PART OF THE MORNING WITH IDBASH. WE HAD
SNACKED ON SOMETHING AKIN TO SHEEP
JERKY—A MEAT I AFFECTIONATELY CHRISTENED
MUTTONJEFF—AND TALKED ABOUT THE UPCOM-
ING CRUSADE FOR THE PROMISED LAND.

Idbash was unmarried and seemed to be saving
his energy for battle. On several occasions while in my
company, he and Ebadiah had discussed strategies for
conquering Canaan. It was difficult not to interject what
knowledge I held, even though it was by no means
that of a Bible scholar. At times Idbash would propose to
do this or that, then look at me as if to say, "Will this work?
Is this wise?" Not wanting to mess with history, I would
respond with something like, "I think Joshua will give you
excellent leadership," or "God hasn't brought you here to
abandon you." In truth, my knowledge contained enough
holes that I might have told them to blow a trumpet at
the Gaza Strip, and God only knows how biblical history

might have been forever changed.

I had been back at my watch only a short time when I saw the unmistakable silhouette of Joshua approaching from the northeast, indicating he'd been visiting my bucolic buddies. I was again struck with this man when I learned he'd come out to personally invite Ebadiah and Idbash to Moses' last sermon. I suppose it was his way of thanking them for baby-sitting me for the past couple of months, but I was not at all surprised when he described their enthusiasm and gratefulness.

"Ebadiah and Idbash are good men," I said to him. "Joshua, I have to admit I'm really in awe of you. I'm sure you've probably noticed my admiration. You're a class act."

"Thank you, Brad," he said. "That's kind of you to say. It's important to me to see that each person feels valued. The small amount of time it takes to recognize people is usually the best investment you can make. If you're sincere, you'll reap a multitude of rewards."

"You know, Joshua, maybe I'll just stay here after all," I said appreciatively.

"Is the future such an inconsiderate place?" he asked.

"On any given day," I answered.

Thinking aloud, I changed the subject. "Joshua, Moses is going to die very soon."

"Moses is old, Brad. He can't live forever."

"No, I mean *soon*," I reiterated. "I think he's in his last month."

"Are you certain?"

"Yes. I know it's not good for me to reveal what I know about the future, but I want you to know this. If there's any advantage for you, I want you to have it."

"Brad, Moses already knows he won't be crossing the river with us—God's revealed that much to him. But a month is not much time. Have you told him?"

"No," I replied. "He's held tight to not asking, but I think he senses it."

"Moses understands things in ways you and I never will. Don't lose sight of that, Brad." He put his hand on my shoulder and offered a reassuring smile. "I'll see you tomorrow for the final message from our beloved friend."

"Our beloved friend," I echoed.

I pursued sleep that night, but it outmaneuvered me whenever I came close enough to be a threat. I wondered if I should have told Joshua about the Urim and Thummim, wondered if he would have offered to help me attempt to get home. I thought of Eve and wondered whether she'd made a second effort to retrieve the other oracle. It had been a week since I'd seen her, and while the passing time didn't specifically give me cause for concern, what she was planning to do certainly did. But tomorrow was Moses' final appeal to Israel. Nodding off during the message would surely not be kosher. I simply *had* to get some sleep. After solving all of the ancient world's problems, I finally succumbed.

A few abbreviated hours later, my eyes popped open as if spring-loaded. A chilly reminder of the crisp desert night nipped at my extremities, and a weary ambivalence pervaded my thoughts. I was tired. My brain and my body cursed me when I ordered them to attention, yet I knew I had to go. I had to be there. At this point, any other choice would be nothing short of lunacy. I shook off the blankets and got up.

"Come one, come all," I said in my best ringmaster's voice. "Ladieeees and geeeentlemen, boys and girrrrls, you're invited to the third sermon of Deuteronomy. A speech by Moses that will be forever treasured in the hearts of all Jews and one tired, confused, displaced Gentile." I threw on my garment, sandals, and trusty sunglasses, picked up my staff, and headed for Nebo.

The trek was remarkably invigorating, shaking me from my morning funk. Old Testament Ammon was no place for a night owl, but conditions had dictated my rather unfriendly schedule since I'd arrived here. I was growing progressively anxious to reverse that tide.

The sun's first feeble rays had just decided to tease the packed sand as I set out. In the distance, a leathery cobra stretched sluggishly toward the foothills, lifting his hooded head as if to make himself appear taller. I'd encountered many of his siblings over the past weeks and had come to appreciate them. My shepherd's crook was always ready to give them a nudge if their curiosity or sense of peril brought them a little too close. Idbash and Ebadiah never killed them, saying that snakes have to make a living like everyone else. It made sense to me.

Closing in on Hebrew Bandstand, I realized that I had arrived much too early—or so I thought. I saw only two figures near the mountain's edge. But a few dozen yards later, I realized my tending partners, like the proverbial kids going fishing, must've made the trip in the dark.

"Some guys just have to get the best seats," I called out

as I sauntered within hearing distance. "Why didn't you wake me, and we could've walked here together?"

"You were snoring when we reached your tent," Ebadiah said in a barely audible voice. "We figured a little extra sleep couldn't hurt you."

"A *month's* sleep wouldn't hurt me," I responded. "How long do you have to watch sheep and goats around here to qualify for a paid vacation?" Idbash looked at me strangely, and Ebadiah began to smile.

"Wherever you're from must be an interesting place," he said. "You can actually be paid for staying home?"

"It's a perk," I answered. "That's short for *perquisite*. It's a benefit, a reward you get for being loyal."

"But isn't loyalty a reward in itself?" asked Idbash.

I looked at the ground for a long moment, then back at Idbash. "Yes, it is. It surely is," I said, feeling that even the cobra I'd just seen could look down at me. Ebadiah wisely changed the subject, and we soon found our box seats. As the rest of Israel's race began streaming in, my friends shared their accounts of Joshua's visit. My spirits rose with their joy, and the sun's neighborly trek across a land that only *seemed* to be Godforsaken helped prepare me for what was to come: the very best of Moses.

The throngs seemed prescient, ready to celebrate. Young children smiled and fought their mothers for freedom, winning the right to romp with their cohorts. Young men, soon to be carrying swords and spears toward Canaan, wore their pride like badges of honor. *If I had a few cases of No Fear T-shirts,* I thought to myself, *I could move up the social ladder in Ammon overnight.*

This was Israel's day; they had pondered their psycho-
logical spanking from Moses for the past week, and the
time-out was over. They would devour this conclusive pep
rally and then head down the tunnel to emerge in the
ultimate Super Bowl, the battle for the Promised Land.

The masses were eager. When Moses and Joshua
stepped up on the bedrock stage, the roar that bounced off
Nebo must have echoed all the way to Jerusalem. I stood
and clasped the raised hands of my friends, Idbash on my
left, Ebadiah on my right. Three shouting shepherds saluted
a man who had given every atom of his being for his God
and his people.

"Mo–ses! Mo–ses! Mo–ses! Mo–ses!" He raised his arms
to quell the ovation, but this time the crowd would have
none of it. The cheers seemed to swell to a cogent thunder.
Although I wasn't close enough to be certain, I thought I
saw Moses begin to smile.

It was Joshua who now stepped forward to request
decorum. After a time, the men with their crude megaphones succeeded in their quest to silence the revelers. All
eyes and ears were now the property of Moses.

"Today," he began with resolve, "you become the people
of the Lord your God!"

The noise began immediately—the shouts, applause,
and tambourines. Wherever people had room to move, they
danced in place, many waving their arms wildly and chan-
neling every drop of energy through their vocal cords. With
the temperature rising from a combination of Heshbon heat
and tightly packed bodies, I watched and waited for the first
sunstroke victim. (What I'd failed to consider was that we

were still in late spring; these people were acclimated to *summer*.)

"Look around you," Moses began once again. "Look at the leaders of your tribes. Look at your elders, your officers, your soldiers. Men, look at your wives and children. Look, Nation of Israel, upon who you are! Now look at the stranger in your camp, he who chops wood for you, he who carries your water.

"Today you enter into a sacred agreement with God, and God shall make you a people unto Himself, a holy people. Just as He promised our fathers Abraham, Isaac, and Jacob, He claims you for His own—all those here and all those who are part of our nation. Look at yourselves, O children of the great and Almighty God!"

We rose again, and there were tears of joy, laughter, and earfuls of happy noise. This was catharsis defined.

"Today I offer you the law of life, the good and truthful words of God. Obey them, and the fruits of heaven will be yours. I command you then to love the Lord, to walk in His paths, and to keep His statutes that you may live and multiply bountifully in the land He is giving you.

"There is nothing so mysterious about this that it cannot be understood. It is not as if it is a secret hidden in the heavens, so that you would ask, 'Who will go up and bring it to us?' Nor is it across the sea, so that you would wonder who would brave the billows to retrieve the message. No! Indeed the Lord has written the words on your very hearts. See that they remain there always.

"I call heaven and earth as my witnesses. I have set before you the path of truth, the ways of blessing—and

I have already warned you of the dangers of arrogance and pride. Choose life, Israel. Choose life!"

There was another eruption, an affirmation of Moses' appeal, and the old sage raised his arms as if in humility. He was already tiring—I knew that—but he wasn't finished.

"I stand before you as a man who is 120 years old. I can no longer lead you. God has revealed to me that I will not cross the Jordan. Therefore hear, O Israel, as I commission the man God offers in my stead."

Moses turned slowly to his right, extended his arm, and beckoned Joshua to his side. As soon as he was close enough, the old man reached out and placed his hand on Joshua's head.

"To you, Joshua, who have been both as a son to me and a surrogate father to this nation, I place the commission of Almighty God. Lead by His might, His will, and His power, and you shall not fail. Be strong and courageous, never be afraid, never doubt, for God travels with you wherever you go. O Israel, I give you your new leader, Joshua."

As the multitudes shouted through tears of elation and sadness, Moses embraced his successor, his friend. I couldn't help wondering how it must feel to pass on the hopes and dreams of a lifetime to another man.

Moses raised his hands one last time, and the silence was almost instantly unbearable. He leaned over and said something to Joshua, who embraced him one final time. Then Joshua headed down through the Hebrew masses toward the west. The crowds parted like the Red Sea as he passed through, and many of the people bowed. After several minutes, he had reached a plateau on the other side, where he stood, waiting.

"Turn around, Israel," shouted Moses. "Turn around." The unsure crowds slowly consented. "There stands Joshua, your new guide. Follow him, trust him, obey him—for God has molded him to lead you. He will take you into the Promised Land that you now face. Look, my children! Look! There, across the Jordan, are the footprints of God!"

Moses had cast the mold, framed the picture: The Promised Land lay ahead, and God was already there. Joshua stood at the helm, and the people faced him, ready to follow. Moses had relegated himself to the background. No one was looking at him. No one except me. I bowed my head and wept openly.

THURSDAYS WITH MOSES

chapter eighteen

THE URIM:

CALLING ON AN OLD FRIEND

I'M SURE I WAS THE FIRST TO LEAVE NEBO, WALK-
ING IN SOLITUDE BACK TO MY TENT WHILE THE
NATION OF ISRAEL REMAINED BEHIND TO RESIDE
IN THE MOMENT AS LONG AS POSSIBLE. THE SUN
SUGGESTED THAT IT WAS BARELY NOON, AND THE
REST OF THE DAY WOULD BE MINE. I WAS
ALREADY MENTALLY DRAINED, AND THE IDEA OF
JUST CRAWLING INTO MY TENT AND DYING FOR
TEN OR TWELVE HOURS SOUNDED ALMOST AS
GOOD AS A PEPPERONI PIZZA AND AN ICE-COLD
PEPSI. AS IF I HAD A CHOICE.

Seeing my dilapidated canvas cottage in the distance, I
began to let down. The first American zombie of Ammon, I
trekked the remaining fifty yards on autopilot and fell into
my shepherd's condo. My mind, body, and spirit torpedoed
into dreamland.

Unsurprisingly, I woke up late in the afternoon, thinking I had really died and gone to a place even hotter than Ammon, which was difficult to imagine. The saunalike atmosphere was beyond breathable, so I got up and headed out for a walk. Having slept four or five hours, I knew I would have trouble sleeping that night if I didn't get some exercise. As if being three thousand years out of sync wasn't bad enough, I had now managed to throw my sleeping pattern to the wolves as well.

I had no desire to head for my tending post; Joshua had seen to it that other tenders were covering for the three of us. Israel was celebrating in its own way, and I wasn't about to go into the main settlement.

I wondered what Eve was doing. For the first time I really pondered where she'd landed here, how she had survived, whom she might be staying with.

I remained confident that as bright, clever, and innovative as she was, Eve was all right. She could improvise, and she looked more like the Hebrews than I did. She could be in the middle of the settlement for all I knew, and that wasn't a place that Moses and Joshua wanted me to go. I decided to head back to the cave and check on the Urim.

The path seemed to smile at me like an old friend, and even the daydreaming lizards and distracted scorpions welcomed me in their own way. I smiled in amazement of the simple, life-changing power of a nap.

At least three or four hours of daylight remained: plenty of time to get to the cave, certify one-half of my tenuous time ticket home, and return before dark. My appointment book had only committed me for Thursdays with Moses and sheep and goats the rest of the time. Even if I got back late, it wasn't like I was going to miss *Sabbath Night Live* on the Hebrew Broadcasting Network.

As I approached the site, I recollected Eve's prank. For a moment, I thought I heard something. I raised my staff and advanced toward the opening, but everything seemed to be fine. I yelled "Hello" loudly, but there was no response. Still prepared for an unpleasant surprise, I stepped cautiously inside the cave.

False alarm. The cave was quiet and serene—and as cold as the frozen-food aisle at Kroger's. *What an incredible gift of nature,* I thought as I sucked in the sixty-degree air. In my euphoria, I'd nearly forgotten my main reason for being there.

Let's see, I said to myself, *the crock should be right over here.* I walked to the spot and looked around but saw nothing. *Not to worry. It must be the other side.* But it wasn't. I traced the front walls as far back as the light would allow and found nothing, absolutely nothing. Closing my eyes, my wife's face appeared vividly in my mind. I wanted to cry again, but Moses had exhausted my day's supply of tears.

chapter nineteen

THE TENTH THURSDAY:

WE TALK ABOUT COMMITMENT

I SPENT THE NEXT FOUR DAYS PRETENDING TO
CARE ABOUT SHEEP AND GOATS. I WAS GOING FOR
THE WORLD'S RECORD FOR MOST CONSECUTIVE
TRIPS ON AN EMOTIONAL ROLLER COASTER. I FIG-
URED WHEN I GOT TO THE NEXT PEAK, I'D JUMP.

When Thursday finally arrived, I didn't even feel like
going to see Moses. Somehow, it all seemed fruitless. Yet that
was our agreement, and the alternative was neither palat-
able nor inspiring. I headed for his tent, first wondering how
I, as depressed as I was, would ever be able to cheer him
up. Then I slipped another notch and questioned whether it
was possible to commit hara-kiri with a shepherd's staff.

I stood outside the tent's door and called Moses' name.
"Come in, Brad," he called in a voice that sounded even
weaker than four days earlier. "Please, come in." I entered and
saw a man who was beginning to look all of his 120 years.

"Come here, my young friend," he entreated. I moved
close to receive an embrace. The odor inside the tent held a
certain unpleasantness, an annoying fragrance that reminded

me of potpourri bathroom spray. In spite of his own circumstances, my host seemed upbeat.

"Moses," I said, "I left part of myself with you back there
last Sabbath. I want to be more like you."

"Do you? Do you really?" he asked.

"You were so unselfish, so willing, so committed."

"Commitment defines us," he stated calmly. "If you are
committed to someone or something—a project, a goal,
anything important—then you must be unselfish. You must
be willing to do whatever needs to be done. I've not always
lived up to my *own* expectations, let alone God's, but I've
tried to remember that it doesn't matter who the leader is
or who gets the glory as long as the task is completed, the
goal is reached."

"When you're beaten down, exhausted, and ready to
quit, how can you stay focused on the goal?" I lamented.

He paused in recollection. "Our people once fought a
battle at Rephidim," he continued, "against Amalek and his
army. God had already tested us, but this had me worried. I
told Joshua and my troops that I was taking Aaron and Hur
with me to the hilltop nearby, while they went to engage the
enemy. I held my staff high to inspire them, but soon my
arms grew tired. I noticed that every time I lowered my
arms, our casualties grew. When I raised them, we were winning. This was when I knew God was watching me closely.

"So I alerted my friends. They sat me down on a large
rock, and each of them supported one of my arms. The
battle lasted all day, and my arms stayed up. We won a
decisive victory."

I said nothing, afraid an incorrect interpretation might

be disheartening for my mentor after so many training sessions. He refused to let me off the hook.

"What does this tell you about commitment, Brad?" he asked.

"It's foolish to go it alone," I responded.

"That's an excellent start," he encouraged. "We could talk about who the real heroes were in this situation, but I think you already know."

"You, your friends, and the army all played their parts," I offered. "But do you think God would have allowed you to lose the battle if you'd simply not lifted your arms because of fatigue?"

"This may surprise you, but I've never really thought about that." His voice elevated, and he became more animated. "Most people spend way too much time trying to second-guess God. I saw what was happening and reacted to it by telling my friends, who responded quickly using their best judgment. If we'd taken the time for a deep theological discussion, our men would have become sliced manna."

"But didn't you say you felt God was watching you?" I asked.

"Exactly!" he answered. "And looking back on it, I'd say He may have just been wanting to see if we had enough common sense to work together to solve a rather simple problem. I think we passed."

"And you did it without a committee, a study, and a vote of the board!" I said.

"Sliced manna!" he repeated.

We shared a moment of laughter before I spoke. "Moses, sharing the load can't be the greatest part of commitment.

Commitment is far too personal. I saw that in your installation of Joshua last Sabbath."

"Sometimes we ask ourselves, *What am I willing to die for?*" he philosophized. "I think a better question might be, *What are we willing to live for?* Day in and day out, what is worth our time, our resources? What are we willing to be consumed by?

"Some are strongly devoted to marriage and relationships, while others are fully engaged in accumulating lands, flocks, gold, and material wealth. It is very difficult—if not outright impossible—to do justice to a spouse, or God for that matter, when one is up to one's ears accumulating possessions.

"As for me, you know my story, what I've tried to accomplish for my people and my God. And while I understand the attraction to material wealth, I know that this life is shorter than the list of Sodom's righteous men. And my life is drawing to a close.

"I can take heart in turning my life's efforts over to Joshua, realizing that many good things will come to pass for my people. I will live on through these generations in a way that is not possible through gold or lands. If this is the reward for honest commitment, it's one I'm very content with. I will die satisfied. Indeed, I will die happy."

chapter twenty

TAKE A LETTER, EBADIAH

EDITING THE INTERVIEW THAT EVENING, I OBSERVED TWO UNUSED YELLOW PAGES REMAINING, AND I RECONSIDERED MY OPTIONS. I NOW FELT IT IMPERATIVE TO FIND EVE. IF SHE HADN'T REMOVED THE URIM FROM THE CAVE, THEN THE ORACLE HAD BEEN FOUND AND RETURNED—OR STOLEN. PERHAPS SHE'D BEEN FOUND OUT AND WAS FORCED TO RETRIEVE THE ARTIFACT. IN EITHER CASE, I DIDN'T WANT TO THINK ABOUT THE POSSIBLE CONSEQUENCES. I FELL ASLEEP RUMINATING ON HOW I MIGHT LEARN HER WHEREABOUTS.

Friday morning, as my four-legged captives grew increasingly inactive with the midday heat of late spring, I decided to abandon my post temporarily to see if Ebadiah might know anything about Eve. He was tipping a flask of warm water to his lips as I approached and seemed both surprised and pleased to see me.

"Good morning, Brad," he said. "Are the animals loafing at the south range, too?"

"No stampede conspiracies in this heat." I grinned. "I think if the big bad wolf comes by, a couple of sheep might just volunteer to be eaten rather than run."

"What brings you here?" he asked.

"Ebadiah, we're friends, right?"

"Of course we are," he responded. "Are you in trouble?"

"Not beyond what you already know," I answered. "What I need to ask you must be held in strict confidence. I don't want anyone to suffer because of me. I need to get in touch with a young woman, and I wondered if you might know about her. She's in her early twenties, has long dark hair, and probably showed up here about the same time I did. I'd think there might have been a small stir like what I kicked up when I got here."

Ebadiah's face read like a digital billboard. Any plan of feigned ignorance would be wasted.

"Is she related to you?" he asked.

"Not by blood," I replied, "but she's the closest thing to a relative I have here. Look, Ebadiah, this is very important. If you can't tell me where she is, can you get a note to her without anyone knowing about it?"

"I believe that can be done. I certainly can't promise, but I think we can get a message to her. I know the man whose family she is serving. I will try."

So Eve was a servant! And I'd thought being a shepherd was a major demotion. I wasn't certain what duties might be encompassed by her job description, but I pictured her

as Cinderella, on her hands and knees scrubbing, with
ornery, cantankerous taskmasters swatting her behind every
time she tried to rest. I thanked my friend and headed back
to my watch with a growing concern for my fellow traveler
from the twenty-first century.

Early that evening, I got back to my tent and picked up
my legal pad and pen. I considered how I might write a
brief message to Eve and still conserve what paper I had
left. I folded a section no more than three inches high,
creasing it back and forth so it would tear evenly. As for the
communication itself, the situation called for caution since
there was no telling who might read it before it got to Eve, if
in fact it ever did. I settled on a couplet:

The woman, Eve, was heaven-sent,
She was the joy of Adam's tent.

I folded the paper in half twice and laid it by my sunglasses. Once again I felt a twinge of hope.

I awoke early Saturday morning with the intent of quickly
implementing my clandestine plan to contact Eve. I'd temporarily forgotten that Saturday equals Sabbath and that
Ebadiah and Idbash were being replaced for the day. I'd
have to wait at least another twenty-four hours, and my
patience was running about as long as a Middle East peace
accord. I thought about heading toward the settlement, but
my better judgment prevailed. There was no sense in risking
the anger of Moses and Joshua after all this time. Another
sunset without contacting Eve simply meant another day's
seniority for a progressively shiftless shepherd.

At midday on Sunday, I gave the note to Ebadiah. He promised he would do his best to see that she received it without undue attention. It was all I could ask. I could only bide my time and hope she visited my tent as soon as she was able. There are times when you mail a letter or make a call, and you know there's little more you can do—all that remains is to wait on some kind of response. Ebadiah was not E-mail or overnight express, but he was a friend. I had to trust him and focus any residual energy I could muster toward staying positive. At this point, even the slightest hint of confidence was a victory.

THURSDAYS WITH MOSES

chapter
twenty-one

THE ELEVENTH
THURSDAY:

WE TALK ABOUT FORGIVENESS

B the time Thursday rolled around, I'd really expected to hear from Eve, by hook or by crook, but I hadn't. I determined that if something had happened to her, I would find out what and who'd done it, and—since it was beginning to appear that I had little to lose—I would seek justice. As hard as I was trying to emulate Moses, I seemed to be growing more frustrated and disconsolate. Regardless, it was again time for our Thursday tête-à-tête.

When I got to the tent, Joshua was standing outside, and his presence raised my spirits a little. He looked at me with a warm but serious face. "He's resting, Brad," he said, "but he still wants to talk with you."

"I won't stay long," I replied.

"Don't worry," he said. "I think Moses will let you know when he's ready."

"Thanks."

He held open the canopy as I entered the tent. My old comrade was reclining on a pile of blankets and cloth. The unpleasant aroma was even more acute, impressing upon me the value of our remaining moments together. I walked over to his bed and sat on the floor beside him. I took his hand. It seemed frail, a pale bluish ghost of the hand that had clasped mine just a month ago.

"Hello, Moses," I said softly. He squeezed my hand more firmly than I thought he was capable of. "Are you up for this?"

"I am still very much living and breathing," he said in a weak commander's voice. "As long as that remains the case, we shall continue." The corners of his mouth fell well short of their attempt to reach his cheekbones. He looked at me squarely. "God has revealed to me that only a fistful of sunrises are yet mine. I want to share what's weighed on me these last few days as I face the end of my life."

"I have plenty of paper left," I offered, blatantly violating my personal pledge to be honest with Moses. In my denial, I grudgingly hoped the thought might extend his remaining time.

"Forgiveness," he said. "No one should go to his grave without forgiving others. You know, I've told you some stories about my people, about missing out on Canaan the first time around. The men responsible for all that have been gone quite a while now, and I'm finally forgiving them once and for all. I didn't see what they saw. I'm made differently than they were. As angry as they made me then, I'm letting it all go."

"And the extra forty years?" I added.

"In the course of eternity, it means nothing. The forty

years was *my* issue. I knew my time here was limited, and I wanted to see the fruits of my labor. That was selfish on my part. God can do whatever He wants, in His own time. The most generous man is the one who plants a tree, knowing he will never sit in its shade."

He closed his eyes and exhaled a long sigh. "I was upset with Aaron and everyone about the golden calf, but I was up on the mountain so long. I knew in the back of my mind that my people weren't abundantly endowed with patience and faith; they were questioning God just days after He'd performed miracles in front of their noses. I'm taking my share of the blame and letting them all off the hook. I refuse to take that to my grave.

"God has told me I will not enter the Promised Land because of what seems to me to be a minor act of disobedience. But who am I to question Him? He's told me He will show me the land. That's more than those who died in the wilderness ever got to see. If that's my lot, then so be it. I could do much worse than die after standing on a mountain and having God show me where my people's victory will come—where God's promise to us will be fulfilled."

His eyelids closed again. I thought he'd fallen asleep, but as I attempted to slowly release my grip on his hand, his eyes opened, and he began more slowly.

"Perhaps I've spent too much of my time being angry and frustrated. I've always had a picture in my mind of how I thought things should be, of how I thought God wanted things to go—and when people or circumstances altered my plan, it was easy to become upset.

"I'm convinced my anger seldom accomplished anything. I should have forgiven those people sooner—if not for them, for myself and the betterment of my people." He paused again, drawing a breath. "But now I'm near the end, and I have a new appreciation for my own human imperfection. I know that I've tried. I hope my people know that, too."

"They do, Moses. Of course they do," I said, working to conceal my tears.

He struggled to raise himself higher on his makeshift bed, then fell back and rested again. "So you know what I'm going to do?" he finally asked with a flickering gleam in his eyes.

I stared back at him.

"I'm going to forgive myself," he said.

I laid myself gently over his chest and kissed him softly on the cheek. He smiled, closed his eyes, and fell asleep.

I sat at his side for several minutes, staring at this worn, tired warrior, whose words had once again penetrated my conscience like a well-pointed spear. *God can do anything He wants.... I should have forgiven them sooner.... Perhaps I've spent too much time being angry and frustrated.* I determined to let the lessons change me once and for all. Whatever happened to me now, I would take in stride. I made quick notes on my legal pad, wanting more than anything to copy Moses' words verbatim. When I had finished, I looked again at my withering friend and back at my legal pad. One page left.

"He's sleeping," I told Joshua as I exited the tent. "He just told me he's forgiven everyone, including him...including himself." Tears blurred my vision, and I covered my face with my right forearm and began to cry like a child who'd just dropped his ice-cream cone on the ground.

Joshua walked over to me and put his arm on my shoulder. "I'll walk with you for a ways." We headed in the direction of my tent.

"The words of a dying man hold the secrets of life," he said. "And when you realize the man is Moses, how much more we should listen. If God allowed me such a long life, the wisdom I might offer at its end would be babble in comparison. If his insight cuts to your soul, it tells me two things: You're human, and you're listening."

"I'm not ready to lose him," my voice trembled.

"None of us are, Brad. Believe me, I've spent many nights crying, and you saw how the people were torn when he affirmed me as their new leader. But it's time. It's time for a new chapter. We must move forward. God has spoken, Moses has obeyed, I have obeyed, and you must accept what is to be. You have to have faith."

"The magic word," I said. "I need more."

"No one ever has all they think they need," he responded. "Not even Moses, but he had enough. I'll have enough, and so will you."

"Thank you, Joshua. If anyone can follow after Moses, you are that man."

His smile reflected maturity. "He's set the standard pretty high, but all of us answer to a higher call."

"Next Thursday, Joshua. If anything happens in the meantime, will you—"

"I'll be there next Thursday, and so will Moses. He has special plans for that day—come as soon as you wake up."

I looked at him quizzically. "Yes," I said. "I'll come early." *Special plans.* The light went on, and I suddenly felt as if I'd just been invited to join Abraham Lincoln and his wife at Ford's Theatre for the evening production of *Our American Cousin.*

chapter twenty-two

FAITH

MY TENT WAS NOW IN SIGHT, AND THE EARLY AFTERNOON SUN WAS SO INTENSE, I SWORE THERE WAS A KID STANDING BEHIND A ROCK WITH A MAGNIFYING GLASS, FOCUSING THE BEAM ON THE BACK OF MY NECK. MY GRIEF HAD DRAINED ME PSYCHOLOGICALLY, AND I FIGURED MY SUB COULD DO AN EXTRA COUPLE OF HOURS OF SHEPHERDING DUTY. I NEEDED A NAP. I WHIPPED OPEN THE RIPENED CANVAS DOOR AND FELL INSIDE.

"Holy…what the…!"

"Eeahh!"

"Eve! Eve! You're okay!" I exclaimed.

"You scared the devil out of me!" Eve said, trying to regain her dignity.

"The devil is more of a New Testament idea," I taunted, surprised at my flash of intellect. "I didn't do it on purpose! Besides, how was I supposed to know you were in here?" I reached out my arms, and she slid close and hugged me. "Did you get my message?"

"Emily Dickinson and Robert Frost are safe," she teased. "But it was cute and clever. I'm here, aren't I?"

"How long can you stay? Are you in any danger?" I asked.

"I've been here an hour or so already, and that's probably too long," she said. "What's going on?"

"I was up at the cave. The oracle is gone. Did you take it?"

"That's impossible! Tell me you're kidding. Adam, tell me you're kidding!"

"It's missing, Eve. Are you in any trouble? You've got to level with me."

"I'm certain no one saw me take it. If they had, I'd probably be dead by now, don't you think?"

I was relieved. "Yes, I do," I answered, "but I can't imagine what happened to the Urim. I just can't fathom someone stumbling upon it accidentally in such a short period of time."

"What can we do now, Adam? The Thummim is going to be difficult to get, and if they realize the Urim is gone...We have to have both of them. Adam?"

"Eve, we've got to have faith," I said, beginning to believe my own words. "Faith—that's it! We'll come up with something. But for now, you need to get back to where you need to be." I hesitated. "Eve, I'd feel a lot better about our chances if I knew where I could find you."

She seemed relieved. "I wish I could tell you, Adam; I really wish I could. I'm just afraid that might only complicate things even more."

"It's okay." I quickly retreated, not wanting to upset her further. "Meet me here next Thursday afternoon.

Get here any way you can."

We stood up, and I looked into a face that now seemed to reflect trust, like a teenage daughter who just realized maybe her father knew more than she ever cared to admit. And even though she'd thought it unwise to divulge her whereabouts, I was convinced her reasons now had nothing to do with any doubts about my intentions or desire to help her. I also had an inkling that I finally knew something she didn't—though I wasn't quite certain what it was. Perhaps it was the secrets of a dying sage beginning to take shape in his student. Though the classroom was in the ancient past, the instructor had provided timeless answers.

"Be careful, Eve," I said as she turned to leave. "We're going to be okay."

"Adam ate the apple, too," she said, all too seriously.

"So he did." I grinned. "But they both lived to tell about it."

chapter twenty-three

A FRESH PERSPECTIVE

JUST A COUPLE OF HOURS INTO MY FRIDAY MORNING WATCH, I TREKKED OVER TO EBADIAH'S POST.

"Any extra water for a choking friend?" I asked.

"Always," he consented pleasantly, handing me a flask.

"You're an effective messenger. I owe you a favor. Is there some way I can repay you?"

"It wasn't difficult," he replied. "As I said, I know her master."

I went fishing for more information. "Very far into the settlement?"

"I'd rather not say, Brad. I don't want to violate a trust. Suffice it to say that there was not a problem in delivering your communication."

"I understand. Thank you." I was disappointed. I figured knowing exactly where Eve was could prove to be a great advantage. "You can never have too much information," my former boss used to say. I had yet to see him proven wrong on that count.

"Are you going to join our army?" Ebadiah asked with a smile. "You know we'll be crossing the Jordan soon."

"Yeah, I've been training by throwing stones at the sheep. I think I'm ready for the serious stuff." The sound of his laughter was a fair reward as I headed back to my post.

The animals under my care looked different when I returned. They seemed friendlier, happier to see me. The goats that had been indifferent wanted to be petted, and the sheep asked me to listen to their stories. For the first time, I did.

Late Wednesday I walked to the far north post to see Idbash. The unyielding sun of the last few days was pondering capitulation to an approaching cavalry of foreboding clouds, the first of which had already made a favorable impression on the temperature. Subsequently, my hike became nearly enjoyable.

"Have your herds decided to govern themselves?" Idbash called out when he saw me.

"They cast lots yesterday," I answered. "The goats won and told me I had until sundown to vacate the premises. How goes it, friend?"

"I'm just biding my time, waiting to cross the river," he offered. "It can't happen soon enough for me."

"You'll be an excellent soldier," I told him. I meant it. "I would feel secure knowing you were fighting beside me."

Idbash looked surprised. "Do you mean that?" he asked.

"Absolutely," I said with all the honesty in my bones. "Israel is in the hands of good and capable men, and you are surely one of them."

"Thank you, friend," he said. "Thank you."

"What do you make of this sky?" I asked.

"The late spring storms of Ammon are few, but they are not good. Fortunately they pass."

I planted my hand firmly on the shoulder of my companion. "This storm will also pass then," I said.

At night the approaching squall made my tent a nervous wreck, and just when things began to quiet a little, another gust would backhand the wearied fabric. I was glad I'd made the trek to visit Idbash, for not only did I see my friend, but I'd worn myself out. In spite of what was coming, I managed to fall asleep.

I have always been prone to dream, and it is a rare morning that I've awakened without recalling vivid subconscious productions. I'd probably dozed but a spoonful of minutes before the Freudian frames began spinning their impromptu yarns on my tired, defenseless brain.

chapter
twenty-four

THE DREAM

I WAS STANDING ON THE SIDE OF THE JORDAN, LOOK-
ING ACROSS THE RIVER AT JOSHUA WHO WAS SHOUTING
AT ME, "GET IN THE BOAT. COME OVER IN THE BOAT!" IT
WAS AFTERNOON, BUT THE SKY WAS LOOKING DREAD-
FULLY DARK, AND LIGHTNING WAS BEGINNING TO FLASH.
A BURGEONING WEST WIND WAS BEGINNING TO ROIL
THE WATER AS I LOOKED OUT AT THE SMALL, PRIMITIVE
WOODEN CRAFT AND WONDERED IF IT WAS SAFE.

The next scene revealed Eve on board screaming, "I'm sinking! Help me!" I tried to run toward her, but my feet were buried in mud. I was unable to move. Then I saw Moses, float-ing in the air just above me. "Faith," he cried. "Faith will save you!" When I looked back, Eve was gone.

Somehow freed, I ran to the water's edge, and looking back across the Jordan, I saw neither Joshua nor Moses, but instead my home in Michigan. I was sure I saw my family looking out the picture window, motioning for me to come in from the rain, but I would still have to cross the river.

I awoke to a downpour and lay there knowing Thursday morning was furtively edging its way toward my tent. There was nothing I could do to stop it.

chapter twenty-five

THURSDAY:

THE MOUNTAIN, PERSPECTIVE,

AND PEACE

I HAD NO IDEA HOW MANY CATNAPS CONSUMED THE FEW REMAINING HOURS, BUT I SNAPPED OUT OF THE LAST ONE LIKE A NERVOUS TWITCH. IT WAS STILL DARK OUTSIDE BUT NOT DARK LIKE NIGHT. INSTEAD IT WAS OSTENSIBLY THE EARLY PART OF A TENEBROUS DAY. I DRESSED AND SET OUT FOR MOSES' TENT, FEELING AS THOUGH EVERY STEP HAD BEEN PREDESTINED, THAT FATE WOULD DICTATE EVERY-THING I SAID AND DID ON THIS DAY. EVEN THE LIMITED SENSE OF POWER AND SUPREMACY I SOMETIMES FELT BASED ON MY KNOWLEDGE OF THE FUTURE FAILED ME.

The hard, dampened sand crackled beneath my sandals, and above me, cumulonimbus clouds rubbed their hands together, anxiously awaiting the additional heat needed to perform their inclement cantata. I walked purposefully, trying hard to appreciate the place, the moment in time. I knew the inevitable was impossible to change, yet I refused to release my last ray of hope, no matter how futile.

Soon I saw two gladiator-sized men standing in front of the tent. Drawing closer, I recognized them as the bodyguards on duty when I had first arrived three months earlier. Unlike that first meeting, they seemed benign, even friendly.

"Good morning." I saluted. "How is Moses doing?"

"Come and see," one of them responded. "He is waiting for you." The other lifted the canvas door, and I stepped in. The all-too-familiar scent struck me again with a renewed intensity, and I turned to see Moses, fully dressed and sitting up, with Joshua by his side.

"Now that you're here, we can begin our journey," Moses said with a weak yet determined voice.

"Journey?" I echoed in surprise.

"God has offered to show me the Land of Promise today, and it's never good to keep God waiting," he clarified with a wink and a smile that signified the fire in his belly had a residual ember.

"Are you up for this?" I asked naively, knowing full well this was part of the story. "The weather is not looking friendly."

Joshua looked at me as if to say, *Let's do this now,* and I stepped to the other side of Moses to help him up.

"Things that are meant to be cannot be avoided, my friends," he said. "God eventually will step in and see to it. Would you get my sandals for me?"

I bent down to retrieve them, and without rising, gently placed them on his aged feet. When I stood, he rested his left arm on my shoulder, and with Joshua on his right, we angled our way out of the tent and headed resolutely down the path toward Nebo.

The clouds toyed with us. When we first exited the tent, I half expected to see the four apocalyptic horsemen or at least a half dozen funnel clouds. Just a few minutes later, the sky lightened a bit, and it seemed possible that we might survive the trip.

"Moses," I said, "why do you think God asked you to climb this mountain today? You could have done this years ago."

"Brad, first of all, the three of us know that I won't be making the return trip." He spoke slowly, pausing often to take a breath. "You probably knew this when you arrived here, and Joshua and I know that God had planned this for some time. So be happy for me that I only have to go *up* the mountain." He hesitated again, almost as if waiting for our laughter. A smile was the best I could muster. Joshua offered a thoughtful grin.

"When I get to the top, God has promised to show me the land that will be ours; then I will rest with my fathers. I will die on the top of that mountain—today." We stopped, and Joshua gave us each a flask of water. It was getting warmer, and the sky seemed to darken again.

"There's more to this, Moses," I said. "Joshua has encouraged me to have faith, and I'm really trying. But God is calling you to the top of a mountain—to die."

"Would you rather die on a mountain peak or on the floor of a valley?" Moses asked, assuming his teacher's role once again.

"On a mountain, of course," I answered.

"And why is that?" he continued Socratically.

"The view is better. You can see everything."

"Perspective," Moses clarified. "From Nebo's peak I will get a glimpse of God's point of view. I will see where we are and where we will be. I will see my own ragged tent and the settlement of my people. How often does one allow God to call them to a place where one can overlook his own life, his own possessions, his own essence? When God shows me what He wants me to see, I will begin to grasp His perspective on the world I've known, its greatness and its smallness."

I was quiet for a long time after this, contemplating the seeming contradiction of life being at once great and small. From Nebo's pinnacle, the lives of important men would seem insignificant; from God's viewpoint, should *anything* on Earth really matter? As if my sadness over Moses' impending death wasn't enough, now these thoughts troubled me as well.

Joshua had been amazingly mute, like a guard at the Tomb of the Unknown Soldier. He appeared to be focused only on the mission at hand. I knew better. He had been Moses' right hand for a generation, and he was positioned there now, helping his mentor up the road to his mountain-top grave. He was surely feeling this more than I; yet he also knew the mind of his dying comrade much better than I ever would. I was still the student. While it appeared that this was my last day of school, Joshua had graduated summa cum laude from this institution years ago—then gone on for his Ph.D.

The foot of Nebo grew closer.

I saw the first flash of lightning behind the mountain to the southeast and the faint rumble of thunder as if the God of Moses cleared His throat in anticipation of speaking to His moribund servant. We rested briefly and drank again from the flasks. I needed an answer.

"If God has the perfect vantage point, Moses, what do you think He finds significant here? Don't we look smaller to Him than the men of Israel will look to you from Nebo's peak?"

"The key is in your words," Moses counseled. "Do human

155

beings ever have a *perfect* vantage point? Of course not! Our
perspective is always clouded by our opinions, our lack of
knowledge, our selfishness, our limited vision. Therefore, don't
believe that even the tallest mountain will offer any man a
genuinely Godlike perspective. It's only a beginning, because
all things that look great from below look equal from up there."

"Okay, so we start with everything being equal," I agreed.
"How can we be sure that we even matter?" I had one page
to fill and too many questions left to be quiet. Moses
showed no sign of exasperation.

"I know we matter because I've seen God's protection,
heard His voice, and seen His works. Most people have.
They just don't recognize it for what it is. But remember, we
are part of God's creation. Just because people look small
when seen from the top of a mountain doesn't mean God
finds us insignificant. His perfect vantage point always
allows Him to see our importance."

We had reached the foot of Nebo.

"Do you want to continue or rest a while?" Joshua asked
our aged friend.

"Let's continue," he answered. "God may not have all day
to wait on an old man." He turned and winked at me. I smiled
and shook my head in disbelief. One hundred twenty years
old, ready to climb the big hill to the cemetery, and still the
consummate entertainer.

There was a well-worn path stretching uphill as far as I
could see. The hillside was dotted with scraggly, olive-colored
bushes, pretending to offer shelter to the rocks and stones
lying beneath them. The trail did not seem steep physically,
but I wondered if my spirit could survive the climb.

"Moses, you told me last week that you had forgiven

yourself, your enemies, and God. But you also mentioned that you were angry for a long time about not being able to live in Canaan, to join the group that would possess the Promised Land. When you look upon it for the last time, don't you think those feelings will return?"

"It's taken some time, Brad, but by forgiving I've helped secure my own perspective. Once you establish that, you should never, ever look back. It's one thing to fall forward, but don't trip over anything that's behind you.

"Every person who cares about others, who wants to change things for the better, must understand they have a role to play, but there's no promise that they'll share in the final glory they hope to create. God has allowed me a part in freeing my people from slavery. That was my role, and I'm at peace with it. This peace may be a gift of God or simply an understanding I've come to acknowledge. Either way, being at peace with oneself is a good thing. As for the final view, God and I are going to celebrate it together."

It had taken Moses over a hundred years to come to grips with forgiveness, peace, and perspective. At least now I had an excuse: I just hadn't lived long enough.

The storm presently seemed to swirl around the entire mountain, and it appeared to be raining angrily everywhere but Nebo. Ominous clouds lurked above us, growling and cranky but saving their ammunition. This was anything but the perfect day for a bird's-eye view of the landscape, and we weren't far from the summit.

"Let's take another rest," Joshua urged, and we drank again. The final stretch would take but fifteen or twenty minutes.

Moses seemed to be gaining strength with each step, leaning less and less on me for support.

"I'm ready," he stated. "This is my time."

"To everything there is a season," I began, "and a time to every purpose under heaven: a time to be born, and a time to die...a time to plant, and a time to pluck up that which is planted...a time to break down, and a time to build up...a time to weep, and a time to laugh...a time to mourn, and a time to dance...a time to get, and a time to lose...a time to rend, and a time to sew...a time to keep silence, and a time to speak..."

The two men listened intently.

"That's beautiful," said Moses. "Where did it come from?"

"A future king of Israel," I answered. "An Israel that you've begun, Moses, the nation that you've nurtured here in the desert these last forty years."

His face flushed with elation. "Come, my friends," he said. "Let's finish what we've started."

"Moses," I said, just loudly enough to be heard.

"Yes?"

"I need to say good-bye to you. The last leg of the journey belongs to you and Joshua."

"Don't worry too much about perspective, Brad," he suggested. "You're already catching on." He took a step toward me, and I took the next to his embrace. I put my head down into the dampness of the sweat-soiled garment that covered his life-worn shoulder and began to weep.

"There may be a time to cry," Moses said after giving me nowhere near enough time to get the grief out of my system, "but let's not waste too much of it on an old man."

"I'm sorry," I choked out.

"Our time together has been special. I hope you have found it meaningful. Remember, I'm just a man."

"Just a man," I echoed. "Thank you, Moses. You'll be remembered forever."

"Good-bye, Brad. Have faith."

I watched through misty eyes as Moses put his arm upon Joshua's shoulder, and they began the final ascent up the trail.

"Moses!" I called out. They halted and looked back curiously. "Enjoy the view."

He smiled, raised his hand off Joshua's shoulder to wave, then turned back to the path. When I could no longer see them, I walked over to a flat rock the size of a kid's wagon, sat down, and stared into the tempest surrounding this altar on which Moses was placing himself.

I was living the last page. I went over and over his words, coercing my short-term memory to recall them exactly as he'd spoken them. I had promised him I would try to deliver his wisdom to the world of my time, and it was critical to keep it intact. My mind flew like sand grains in the storm.

"Brad! Brad!" It was Joshua's voice, calling from just above me. I hurried to the trail and answered. Soon he was at my side, and a glance at his face told me that his final moments with Moses had also been emotional ones.

The thunder grew so loud that I had to shout, "Should we stay up here or go down now?"

"Let's move toward the west side!" he shouted.

"I'll follow you!" I bellowed as loudly as I could. I thought we *were* on the west side, but apparently the trail had wound around to the south. I was no Boy Scout. Without the sun or a decent view of the land below, I was as useless to Joshua as a pork dinner.

He motioned for me to hurry and gestured toward a small stand of emaciated trees that were steadfastly attempting to open some tiny purple blossoms. We sat on the ground beneath them, facing west toward the Jordan, and waited.

The wind's roar now seemed to fall behind us to the east, and the veil of darkness across the river began to lighten, first as if amber streetlights were coming on slowly in a fog, then stronger and more intensely. A bright beam began to pour through the blackness from high in the eastern sky. I knew it had to be the sun, but I could've sworn it was in the wrong location.

As we watched spellbound, the blackness encompassed everything but the view west: the Holy Land. The sun, like a solitary, exuberant spotlight, focused its effervescent rays on the place of milk and honey, the inheritance of Abraham's race. We were witnessing the original version of *Fantasia*—three millennia before Disney.

For a brief but timeless moment, the wind and rain stopped, and it seemed as though the light of fifty suns was focused across the river. Then the din of thunder began, and I was sure I heard a voice in the wind say, "Well done, Moses, well done." I looked at Joshua as if to ask whether I was hearing things. His stare confirmed he'd heard it, too. The sun disappeared again, and a thick ebony vapor enveloped the summit. It swirled and lifted as quickly as it had fallen, then evaporated into the heavens. The sun broke through once again.

"Moses is dead," Joshua said.

We stared up at the peak for several minutes, until at long last, Joshua turned and started the descent down Mount Nebo. I followed silently. It was unthinkable to come down without Moses. By the time we reached the bottom, any evidence of bad weather was negligible.

"Looks like this storm is over," declared Joshua.

"So it appears," I offered, knowing my own uncertainty remained. "What would you like me to do now, Joshua?"

"Go back to your tent and rest," he said. "Our bodies and our souls have been taxed today. And, Brad..."

"Yes?" I looked at him questioningly.

"Get that last page right." He smiled, but I knew he meant it. He sat down on a rock, and I headed back to carry out his wishes—something I knew must be done before I could entertain any thought of sleep. I popped into my tabescent tepee, plucked up my pen, and inked the final glory of Moses on the remaining yellow page, closing with, "As for the final view, God and I are going to celebrate it together." I knew I had it nailed.

Moses was right, I said to myself. *He and God had one incredible celebration.*

I'd lost all track of time. When the canvas door of my tent flew back, I nearly shed my skin. Eve appeared in the doorway. "Don't you ever answer your E-mail?" she quipped.

"Eve, 9-1-1 doesn't work out here, and defibrillators won't be around for another three thousand years. If you're truly bent on sending me into cardiac arrest, let me write a note for you to take to my wife explaining how I died."

"You told me to get here any way I could, so I'm here. What's going on?"

"Moses is dead."

"You're kidding. How do you know?"

"Joshua and I escorted him up the mountain. As fantastic as our situation is, you still wouldn't believe what I witnessed today."

"I can stay a little while. Tell me." She sat down, and I spent the next hour relating the experience. "Where do you think that leaves us, Adam? Do you have a plan?"

"I want to wait until Sunday," I said. "Joshua is our best hope, and he needs a few days to deal with this. As soon as the Sabbath is over, I'll talk to him."

"Do you know where his tent is?" Eve asked.

"Not for sure. Do you?" I was suspicious. I knew Eve was in the settlement, and Joshua's address probably wouldn't be difficult to discover if I could mingle with more of the Israelites in the camp.

"I have a pretty good idea," she said. "If you need to get a message to him, I can probably help. I need to get back. Are you okay, Adam?"

"Okay? What do you mean?"

"Well, with losing Moses and everything," she said.

"It's changed me forever," I answered. "He tried to teach me so much. I tried to absorb it.... I don't think I did very well."

Eve smiled, and a consoling arm found its way to my shoulder. Once again, I succumbed to tears.

"Get some sleep, Adam," she suggested softly, sounding motherly. I felt a light kiss on my forehead, and she got up to leave.

"The last page is written, Eve. I think something has to happen. Something *has* to happen."

"We have to have faith, Adam. Remember?" She ducked out of the tent and was gone. Looking out behind her, I noticed the sun setting. Time was beginning to feel irrelevant. I tossed myself down on the jumble of stale blankets, and a spent man from third-millennium America once again went in search of the ancient desert sandman.

chapter twenty-six

A MOONLIT DESERT NIGHT:

SALVATION

WHEN MY EYES OPENED AGAIN, IT WAS THE

MIDDLE OF THE NIGHT. IT SEEMED LIKE I'D BEEN

ASLEEP FOR WEEKS, YET I KNEW IT COULDN'T

HAVE BEEN MORE THAN A FEW HOURS. I

REACHED OVER AND FELT THE YELLOW PAD,

AND THE REALIZATION OF ITS FILLED PAGES SUG-

GESTED MY MISSION COULD ONLY BE COMPLETED

WHEN I RETURNED TO PRESENT-DAY AMERICA

AND THE WIFE AND FAMILY I DEARLY LOVED.

A sudden resolve came over me to get home, one way or another. I rifled through the old blankets in the corner of my tent until I had retrieved my Levis, T-shirt, and tennis shoes. They smelled like zoo dust, but I hurriedly donned them anyway and left the tent to find a full moon illuminating a tranquil desert. I thought I was alone—for a moment. Accompanying my skin's first appreciation of the night breeze was my observance of two silhouettes in the distance.

They were apparently coming from the encampment. I headed in their direction.

Moving closer, one appeared to be larger, undoubtedly a man; the other, shorter, trim, feminine. "Who are you?" I called out, exercising caution.

"Friends," a male voice answered, a voice that sounded familiar. I began running toward them.

"Joshua!" I exclaimed. "What on earth are you doing here at this hour?"

"It's the safest time for a walk in the desert," he responded. "I have something for you—a gift from Moses."

Now just a few yards away, I noticed that his companion's face was covered by a veil. "You're kidding," I said in disbelief. "Moses left me a gift?"

"Yes, Brad. I only wish our mutual friend could be here to give it to you in person, but this was what I was instructed to do. Esther. . ." The servant handed Joshua a small, ornate box made of silver. He held it out, and I took it from his hands.

"It's beautiful," I said.

"Open it carefully," he instructed. I lifted the lid and took two turquoise-colored cloth rolls from inside. As I began to unwind the first, my hands began to tremble, and I realized what was happening. I held one of the artifacts.

"The Thummim!" I blurted, seeing the elaborate bull's head staring dauntingly at me. Joshua started to chuckle.

"Actually, that's the Urim," he said. "You had a fifty-fifty chance."

"Joshua, you can't give me these. And besides, I can't leave without Eve."

"Who's Eve?" he asked, obviously surprised.

"A young woman who had the misfortune of being too close to me a few thousand years from now."

"Well, would you take Esther back with you instead?" He lifted her veil to reveal his servant's identity: Eve.

"Esther?" I said, beginning to laugh.

"Eve?" Joshua followed, pushing the knife a bit deeper.

"So you're torn between being first among women and being the most virtuous. Eve, you are truly a piece of work."

Joshua offered a puzzled grin.

"Don't worry," I said. "It'll be another eight hundred years before the real Esther shows up."

"You need to go," he urged. "Under the cover of darkness, you'll be safe. Go back to the cave. I'll check there tomorrow. And don't forget your writing!"

I took three quick steps and threw my arms around him. "This has been amazing, Joshua. Amazing beyond any words I know. You are the new Moses. You deserve everything good."

"Thank you, Brad. Moses will always be the model for heroes. May God watch over you and get you home safely. Perhaps we'll meet again someday." He turned to Eve. "And as for you, Esther—alias Eve—if you ever require work, my servants' quarters will be open. God bless you."

"Good-bye, master," she offered, sounding too much like Barbara Eden for her own good, as she walked to my side. Joshua winked and pointed toward the hills where the cave lay. We turned and headed that way.

"My notes, Eve. I've got to stop at my tent."

Once there I grabbed my legal pad now brimming with Moses' insight, shoved my pen into my back pocket, and exited my sojourner's palace. "I never asked you about your living conditions, Eve, or should I say, Esther?"

"Look, Mr. Museum Klutz, I was being careful. It's still Eve to you."

"Okay, okay!" I backpedaled. "But you ended up as a servant to Joshua. Why didn't you tell me?"

"You should never tell everything you know, at least not without a good reason. Knowledge is an insurance policy when your risk is high—and let's face it, Adam; this is no place for the fainthearted."

"Containment!" I nearly shouted as the epiphany ricocheted in my skull.

"What do you mean, *containment?*" Eve queried.

"I was exiled to this tent and to the herds by the mountains and only able to see Moses for a short time each week at the edge of camp. When I got suspicious, Joshua leveled with me that it was their way of making sure the locals didn't start questioning me about the future. I should have known he was keeping tabs on you, too. You'd think by the time someone reached their forties, they'd figure out the simple stuff."

"You'd think." Eve augmented the injury to my damaged pride.

"Incredible!" I said. "How were you treated?"

"Joshua was not unkind, but this is still a man's world. I'm ready to go home. Do you think we have a chance?"

"Moses and Joshua obviously know more about the power of these artifacts than we do. They also knew about the cave."

"Nothing surprises me here," she answered. "Not anymore."

"We can make the cave in fifteen minutes if we pick up

the pace," I said. "Are you up for a run?"

"Can a guy your age handle the physical challenge?" she taunted.

I broke into a stride, hoping beyond hope that I could outrun her. She kept pace, and by the time I started to slow down three or four minutes later, she wasn't even breathing hard. We slowed to a comfortable jog, and she turned and smiled at me.

"Don't tell me; not only are you clever and charming, but you're also a world-class marathon runner," I said through heavy breaths.

"Don't you remember what I said about having brothers? When you're the only girl, running is essential to survival— especially when you have insightful observations about your siblings and find it impossible to keep them to yourself."

"You? Getting mouthy? I can't fathom it," I chugged out, trying to decide if I should laugh or throw my foot out to trip her. The glimmer of the Ammon moon caught the corners of her mouth as they reached upward, and her Cleopatra smile beneath dark and sparkling eyes was reward enough for the pain of trying to keep pace with her. The sound of our striding bodies defied the absolute silence of the desert, and we were content to be quiet and appreciate the spirit of this last trek across the sands of antiquity.

Soon we were nearing the cave. "If something jumps out this time," I said, "I'm getting behind you."

"You're my hero, Adam," Eve offered with her usual excellent timing and intuitive sarcasm. She reached over and took my hand, and we made our way to the entrance. "Whatever happens," she said, becoming serious, "I want you to know that I appreciate what you did back there."

"Back where?" I asked.

"Back there with Joshua, when you told him you couldn't leave without me. I know you've treasured your time with Moses, but I also know you want to get home as badly as I do. To know you wouldn't leave without me, well, it's kind of overwhelming."

"Seems like I remember promising you we were in this together," I said.

"People have made promises to me before," she answered.

"This is a land of promise," I countered. "It's best to keep it that way." We stopped at the cave's mouth, and by the moon's glow I unwound the cloth from the Urim and handed it to Eve.

"What are you doing?" she asked.

"You'll see," I responded, unwrapping the Thummim. "Let's go." I led Eve by the hand into the cave. Two steps inside, all that was visible were our outlines. "Sit down," I instructed, and we cautiously planted ourselves on the grotto floor. I put the relic into my left hand, shoved my legal pad under my T-shirt, and wrapped my right arm firmly around Eve's shoulder. Understanding, Eve followed my lead, placing the Urim in her right hand. When her trembling left hand settled beneath my rib cage, we were set.

"Are you ready, Eve?"

"Adam, is it okay if I tell you that your friendship has been special to me? Do you know what I mean?"

"I think so," I answered. "You're an incredible woman, Eve, and I can't imagine surviving this without you." I turned my head and gently kissed her cheek. "The future is waiting."

"I'm ready," Eve said, but I felt her apprehension in the hand that now drew hard against my rib cage. I may have avoided any overt signs of fear, and while I knew this was my only possible ticket back to my family and the world I thought I belonged to, a bevy of questions bombarded my thoughts: *What if this doesn't work? Does my wife think I'm dead? How will I get the words of Moses out to the masses? Can I ever live up to all of these lessons? Can life ever be normal again?*

"Here's to the third millennium from now," I said, snapping out of my self-induced fog.

We slowly moved the oracles together, closer, closer... *crack! Fffftt!* A shower of sparks exploded in every direction, and the cave lit up like daylight. Eve screamed, and I felt my left hand burning. I blacked out.

*chapter
twenty-seven*

REALITY

THE ACRID SMELL OF ISOPROPYL ALCOHOL SWIRLED IN MY NOSTRILS, AND MY SUBCONSCIOUS FOUGHT DESPERATELY TO REMAIN IN DREAMLAND. THERE, I WAS SITTING ON THE EAST BANK OF THE JORDAN, DANGLING MY FEET IN THE COOL-BUT-MURKY WATER, WHILE JOSHUA AND MOSES SAT ON EITHER SIDE OF ME, REFRESHING MY SPIRIT WITH ETHEREAL CONVERSATION. I HAD SURELY DIED AND GONE TO HEAVEN.

Much too soon, my sleeping self capitulated, and my eyelids raised slowly up, then down, then up, like a tired GI doing his final push-ups before a demanding drill sergeant. Finally, they locked open, and my mind began to clear.

If the odor wasn't enough of a clue, the dwarfish chrome bars on either side of my bed instantly told me I was in a hospital, and my pulse was readily apparent in my throbbing left hand. I held it up to inspect my fingers, but they were lost somewhere inside a globe of gauze and tape.

Rolling over to my right, I saw a small mahogany stand on which sat an aqua vase holding pink carnations. A picture of

Daniel surrounded by lions hung above, perfectly straight on the beige wall. Sunlight streamed through a tray-sized window three feet to the left. It wasn't a suite at the Hyatt, but for a hospital room, it wasn't bad. I flopped onto my back and stared at the ceiling. I'd probably been in a coma, but I had no idea how long. I heard voices outside the doorway. "Is that room service?" I called out, hoping to see a friendly face.

"My goodness! You're awake! God's grace, but you've had a long nap!" The nurse appeared to be sixtyish, with pretty, gold-rimmed glasses, graying hair, and a grandmotherly manner that made me feel better instantly.

"How long have I been sleeping?" I asked.

"Almost three days," she answered. "We've been worried about you. You survived that earthquake and all, but we don't know why you were unconscious like that. We didn't find any contusions on your head or anything else to indicate why you should have been knocked out. The doctors think your coma might be shock-related."

"I'll do almost anything to get a few extra hours of sleep," I suggested, and she shook her head and laughed.

"What can I get you?" she asked.

"Orange juice would be great," I answered. "Has anyone contacted my wife?"

"They finally got through yesterday," she said. "She should be arriving here anytime now."

"Thank you. You're wonderful. What's your name?"

"Hannon," she said. "And thank you. We're glad to have you as an *awake* patient."

In no time I was sipping cold orange juice, trying to make sense of the video loop rolling over and over in my mind. It had all seemed as real as anything I'd ever done in my life. I just couldn't make myself believe it was the ruse of a traumatized brain.

"Dr. Goldberg asked us to keep him posted on your condition. He's concerned about you. Is it okay if he stops by?"

"Sure," I said. "I'd be happy to see him. Tell him I'm not planning to sue. As far as I know, earthquakes don't fall under the negligence statutes."

"I wish all of our patients woke up as good-natured as you," Hannon bubbled as she left to make the call.

I was baffled about the whole experience and disappointed to think it had all taken place in my head. Still, I was happy to be back, sore hand and all. My growling stomach was a welcome symptom, and shortly Hannon returned taking my order for toast. It had been a long time since breakfast. "Dr. Goldberg is here. May I send him in?"

"Certainly," I answered.

"Thank God you're awake," he offered sincerely.

"How much damage was there?"

"Oh, don't worry about the building. We can repair buildings," he said, almost embarrassed.

"I'm okay, Dr. Goldberg. How bad is the Eretz?"

"We have a lot of damage. We'll be closed for two or three months, if not longer. They're saying that the epicenter was almost directly under our facility. It's unfortunate to be sure, but we're pleased that no one was killed. How is your hand?"

"It hurts, but it'll heal. Do you have any idea what I burned it on?"

"There were some power lines nearby. The doctors said your injury was consistent with an electrical burn."

"I see." I was beginning to wonder again. "Did you find the artifacts?"

"Yes, we were fortunate in that regard as well. As a matter of fact, you had the Urim in your left hand when we found you."

"The copper piece with the woman's head?" I verified.

"Yes."

"That's the Thummim," I said randomly. He looked at me strangely, and I realized what I'd done. "I guess I'm still a little fuzzy," I suggested, covering my tracks.

"Well, I'm sure you need your rest, so I'll be going. I'm pleased to know that you're out of the coma. By the way, I brought your notepad. It wasn't a high priority right after the earthquake, but I picked it up on a sweep through the building yesterday. It looks like you're a prolific notetaker."

"Thank you," I said, clasping the tablet with my right hand.

"My apologies for all of your grief," he offered. "If you ever come back to our city, we'll try to make it up to you."

"Dr. Goldberg, don't apologize for the earthquake. As far as I know, people still call it *an act of God.*"

"Indeed, they still do," he agreed. "My best to you."

"Thank you for coming, Doctor." I extended my right hand for a handshake, and when he gripped it, I felt a twinge of pain. As soon as he exited, I stared at my hands. They'd found the Urim in my left hand, the one that held it in the cave where Eve and I had last been—the same hand that had a nasty burn. How could the hand have contacted electrical wires if it was still holding the oracle? I looked now at my right hand and saw a scar, running tangent to my lifeline.

Wait a minute, I thought. *What did Dr. Goldberg say about me being a prolific notetaker?* I grabbed the legal pad and looked. All of the pages were full—full with the words of Moses! I leafed through, hardly believing what I saw. Near the back of the tablet, the bottom portion of a page had been torn out evenly. I thought my head might explode.

"You're a popular fellow," Hannon said as she popped into the room. "You have another guest, a lady who said she bumped into you at the museum just before the earthquake. May I send her in?"

I stared back at her.

"May I send her in?" she repeated, waving her hand in front of my face.

"Yeah," I said, expecting Rod Serling to appear any minute. "Sure."

It was the pretty, black-haired girl from the Eretz, all right.

"Hello," I said. "I'm really sorry if I was rude at the museum. I'm surprised that you'd come to visit me here."

"After all you've been through, there's certainly no need to apologize," she said rather formally. "How do you feel?"

"Pretty good, all things considered. My hand took some electrical current, and I'm weak from my long nap, but I'm not complaining. They say I'll be on a plane headed home in four or five days. Were you hurt at all? It seems like I remember seeing you fall."

"The fall was minor. I was fortunate." She turned toward me, and I noticed a bandage on her right hand.

"What happened there?" I asked, pointing to the injury.

"Second-degree burn," she said. "The doctors aren't sure what caused it." She moved to the side of my bed and handed me a piece of paper. "I'm leaving for L.A. tomorrow morning. Here's my E-mail address." She leaned over, kissed me on the forehead, and winked.

"You take care, Adam."